2024

Writing from Inlandia

AN INLANDIA INSTITUTE PUBLICATION

RIVERSIDE, CALIFORNIA

For more information, write to:
Permissions
Inlandia Institute
4178 Chestnut Street
Riverside, CA 92501

Executive Director: Cati Porter
Editor: Cait Johnson
Book layout & design: Mark Givens

Printed and bound in the United States
Distributed by Ingram

Published by Inlandia Institute
Riverside, California
www.InlandiaInstitute.org
First Edition

2024 Inlandia Creative Writing Workshop Leaders

John Brantingham

José Chavez

Wil Clarke

James Coats

Carlos E. Cortés

Jane Edberg

Ryan Fingerle

Renee Gurley

Stephanie Barbé Hammer

Sebraé Harris

Bonnie Hearn Hill

Minda Honey

Mae Wagner Marinello

JD Mathes

Rose Y. Monge

David Puma

Lydia Theon Ware i

Frances J. Vásquez

Victoria Waddle

Romaine Washington

This activity is supported in part by the California Arts Council, a state agency. Learn more at www.arts.ca.gov.

Contents

Sunrise at Masada

BY SUSAN M. RUMP ABIR
From Finding Home

My children and I are standing together overlooking the Dead Sea in the Judea Desert. It is 4:45 am just before sunrise. Stars are still glistening in their perpetual constellations. While the mountains of Jordan reflect up at us from the blue glass sea below. No-one says a word. We huddle together in the darkness. The desert feels empty here accept for the Acacia tree near us. It is blooming. I smell a mixture of dust and the scent of pollen, honey, and balsam. I take in a slow deep breath to settle myself. We have come to my husband's country and our new home.

Our family arrived a month ago, but my husband and I have been talking about bringing our family to Israel for years. Every so often Dan and I would grow silent at our table, then look at each other and talk about moving to where he grew up into a young man. Would we live in Tel Aviv where he had lived? In our conversations, we never choose a place. I thought of us, our family, as being happy where we were in Long Beach, California: "why would we leave?"

Ein Gedi

Our trip to Masada started from Ein Gedi Kibbutz: a place of history and antiquities, but also a modern nature reserve with the only *inhabited* botanical garden in the world. Nine hundred species of plants live in this rocky place along with a kibbutz and a field school: which is another way to say an environmental education center where conservation projects, and guided bird walks take place. We are staying at the Ein Gedi Kibbutz so I can create something special with my children before they enter their new school in Israel. I am here with them alone. My husband has flown back to the United States to work while I will attempt to settle our family here in Israel.

The dew this morning gently glosses the leaves of the date palms. Birds are beginning to wake and drink. I hear a Desert Tawny owl call from above our heads and fly out from a tall fan palm. The desert is a sandy bare place here, but I notice Crane's bill rising with purple flowers from the earth next to us on the trail to the car. My mother once showed me how to make a pair of tiny scissors out of the plant's green pointy seeds. I think back to when I was a child in Upland, California. This is where I was born. As I recognize the flowers and the long pointed seeds I envision my mother showing me, and I smile. My mom and dad are far from us now in the United States, but as I stand in the desert with my children I feel like we are all overlooking sunrise together.

Ein Gedi is the first place I chose to travel alone with our children since Dan and I arrived to Israel making Aliya with our family in June. We have settled in a small agricultural settlement called Tel Mond. It is mid July. It was in Ein Gedi that I first felt close to the land of Israel. Dan brought me for the first time on our honeymoon on our trip to Eilat. We climbed the canyon to Natal David, watching Nubian ibices balance and move along the ridged rock walls leading to the springs. Then we made our way to the top of the canyon where we entered the blue green natural pools and stood under the waterfall of David.

Masada

The day begins at 2:30 a.m. when I gentle wake up my children to take them to the car. In the parking lot, they are staring at me tired and annoyed. Their faces seem to say "Why are we up in the dark?" I have gathered them into the car to drive us to Masada. This is a special tradition that young people in Israel will do with their classes and my children know very little about this experience as we set off into the desert. As a teacher, I am constantly gathering information about fun things to learn and understand about our world. I am a life long learner and I am hoping to share this with my children. They are grumbling and a little whiney about not knowing where we are setting off since I always share with them in advance what we will do. But this is all new: the trip to Israel to make Aliyah, the new home in the foreign land of their father, and his leaving only a few weeks after we landed to go back to work in the United States. We are all a little unsure of what could be coming next.

When I turn to check on the children again they are asleep on the drive, and several hours go by in the darkness of the desert. There are no cars on the road to Masada accept for us and the desert rising up from either side. The road is snaking around bluffs moving towards Qumran until we emerge following signs to Masada to the place where we will park. When I pull in the three of them wake up.

My daughter Gabrielle is 14. Her long hair touches her shoulders. She has recently made her Bat Mitzvah a journey to read the Torah in front of a congregation of people we have known off and on since the children were young. Some of our congregation doesn't think a girl should read the Torah, and they won't come in the morning to be part of this ritual that my daughter does so well at. Instead they join us for the oneg: a special meal after the reading. It turns out many more people will come to the oneg in the afternoon than expected. Our women's group have to take out extra lox, bagels, and cream cheese to serve. There is a silent feeling of joy for me on this day, my belief that we are accepted here, that fills the kitchen with love. I finally feel I belong.

My sons Micael and Uriel are 10 and 12 respectively. Both of them have short hair cuts they've gotten with their Abba (their dad). My older son Uriel will be studying for his Bar Mitzvah in Israel with a family who lives close by our home. When I take him to their home, I feel their gentleness and know they are a good family to help my son learn.

Sitting in the car at Masada, it occurs to me that I am filling in for being both mother and father to my children. A wave of insecurity sweeps through me, something I didn't feel when I was younger. I am aware of being far from home. How we are migrating to a country I know very little about, and for which I do not fully speak the language. And I am taking the children into the desert by myself.

When we finish getting out of the van and start making our way up the sandy paths, I say, "This area is like an oasis in the desert." And I smile at them.

All three of my children stare at me. The closest experience we have had is staying in Anza-Borrego Desert State Park in California, but all of the children were under ten back then.

"What did you bring us here for?" Micael asks. He is my youngest child, and the one who has been moved around with me the most. He is the one who told me on a particularly difficult day, "Hug mom, hug" and I embraced him. I sense his irritation. I don't feel like I can answer him yet. So instead, I smile at him putting my hand on his shoulder realizing the sun is about to come up.

"Come on you'll see." I urge us. I try to get us to go on before the heat of the day will begin, and before we discover none of this makes much sense yet. It is still too soon.

"Come on let's take a picture. The sun is almost up. When you go to your new school you can tell your friends that you visited Masada at sunrise. It's a really big deal here to be doing this,"

We all stop hiking at the plateau. The children pose standing at odd angles on the trail with their arms crossed, and at least my youngest son frowning. I take the picture of the three of them together just before sunrise. I am feeling so proud of them for getting here and over-coming their own resistance.

The Dead Sea shines with the light of the cresting sun capturing and holding the reflection of Jordan on the other side. Like a piece of glass, the sea is a divider of worlds, of religions, of ways of understanding. And at the same time it unites the common spaces where diverse populations of people coexist safely. This is 2015 before nova, and taking hostages and again fear and death.

Masada's sparseness hides nothing. Its sheer lines and colors developing minute by minute as we stand with each other. Sunrise catches their attention. They turn toward the curvature of the land meeting the sky: a thin yellow and orange light highlights the silhouette.

"Look at the color!" Uriel says noticing the light and my daughter holds her phone up to frame an exposure.

"Mom this is beautiful." And then she questions, "Are we going to hike into the canyon ?"

"We can get into the water at the top if you want. When we return to Ein Gedi" I say. My daughter smiles at the idea. She has brought a new swim suit with her that she likes. The boys make surprised faces at each other and begin to get excited.

"What about breakfast?" one of them asks.

"Why don't we eat and then go? What do you think?" I suggest.

"Oh yeah!" The boys shout and begin to jump.

Here's To You

by Janet Lako Alexander

cowboy at heart
from East Texas
Purple Heart awarded marine
you never spoke, much less bragged,
about either thing

rat pack Dad
loved water skiing
charcoal grilling steaks
driving your Ford Falcon
filled with wife and kids
and blue cigarette smoke

good time Charlie
a better host than owner
at your bar, the Villa
it embarrassed mom, the teacher,
to walk there after school

Charles the wordsmith
you conjured phrases
urged them through hoops
often entertained with them
sometimes carved us up with them

hardscrabble tough luck Chuck
you could make buildings
from scratch
frame and raise a shed
in one day

get-er-done cement mason
I can point to sidewalks
at universities and hospitals,
the brickwork at our old house,
and say "Dad did that"

rained out of your cement job:
after school I climbed
into your yellow and primer red
International Harvester stake bed
the envy of my classmates

you shared your cotto salami
sandwich on cracked wheat bread
two things I was suspicious of
but munched with pride
because they were yours

come help your Dear Ole Dad
unlacing and pulling off
your yellow work boots
stained with concrete
one of my favorite tasks

Summertime Charlie
handing a gin and tonic
to your grown kids
I lift my glass
here's to you, Dear Ole Dad

Axolotl Dreams

by Janet Lako Alexander

Raindrops on my window.
Dreaming, I swim
in a river in the sky.

I rain down in Mexico
to float in the still waters
of Lake Xochimilco.

I swim with axolotls,
mysterious salamanders
with bendy legs and tiny fingers.

Long tails wave
from side to side
as they glide along.

Flashes of green, brown and black
speckled with gold—
some are even pink.

Their heads are like triangles
with a crown of feathery gills
and a small, secret smile.

Gold circles around dark eyes
that gaze at me.
Are they as curious as I am?

The golden sun in my window
wakes me but I remember
and I wonder:
Do axolotls dream like me?

Sueños de Ajolotes

by Janet Lako Alexander

Gotas de lluvia en mi ventana.
Soñando, nado en un río
en el cielo.

Me llueve en México
para flotar en las aguas mansas
del Lago Xochimilco.

Nado con los ajolotes,
salamandras misteriosas
con piernas flexibles y deditos.

Colas largas ondean
de un lado a otro
mientras se deslizan.

Destellos de verde, marrón y negro
moteado de oro—
algunos incluso son rosados.

Sus cabezas son como triángulos
con una corona de branquias plumosas
y una sonrisa pequeña y secreta.

Círculos dorados alrededor
de ojos oscuros que me miran.
¿Son tan curiosos como yo?

El sol dorado en mi ventana
me despierta, pero lo recuerdo
y me pregunto:
¿Los ajolotes sueñan como yo?

Childhood Home

by Margit Andersson

My home was part of a farming community in Sweden, spread out on each side of a valley which had been carved out during the ice age. The farms were small. At the bottom of the valley ran a brook, a remnant of the ice river that had run through the area some thousands of years earlier.

I have to speak of tangibles and intangibles to describe my home where I lived until I was eleven years old. It was an old house, built in the 1800's. We did not have indoor plumbing, nor central heating. I remember a kind of thin moss, or lichen, grew on the walls of the upstairs stairwell because those walls had no siding or insulation. The house was small, but of course to me, it was big enough and it was all I knew. We had three or four cows, chickens, sheep and a pig sometimes. We grew potatoes, oats, barley and rye.

Our life was essentially the same as everyone else's in the area, with the exception of the larger landowners' whose farms had been in the same family for many generations. Most people were Social Democrats in those days, for good reasons, and the "big farmers" voted conservative which I guess was natural too. But there were no overt social conflicts. It was a stable, homogenous community with a church and school at its center.

In my home, as children, we had what we needed, which was food to eat, a mother who hugged us, who listened to us, and who respected us. We learned indirectly, mostly by example, the importance of paying one's debts, of being helpful and to always curtsy, shake hands and say thank you for any gift.

But we had to start helping out on the farm as soon as we were able to. I might have been five years old when my father fashioned a short hay rake for me so that I could be out on the fields with the family in July or August and help gather the hay for our cows' winter fodder. I may have raked some hay, but what I remember more vividly is my dashing in and out of the haystacks, giving a sort of performance for the family and other help during the coffee breaks. Twice during the day my mother would appear carrying a large tray with coffee pot, cups and saucers, and rye bread sandwiches with butter and cold cuts.

We had free time, time to roam the forest and mountain behind our house, and time for swimming in the lake with its sticky clay bottom and yellow and white sea lilies. There were ideas of forest trolls, and of the Invisible Ones, whom my own great grandmother had actually encountered once, and of Elves. And it was easy for us to believe that the elves were indeed dancing in the misty grove in early evening, surrounded by the fragrant white flowering trees. Those trees flowered in the spring just before the lilacs, and later produced edible but extremely sour dark purple berries which we nevertheless ate.

A friend and I liked to go through the local refuse heaps, spending hours on end there, looking for treasure. We must have built up strong immunities to all sorts of bacteria because we were hardly ever sick. Once when I was three years old, my mother found me sitting contentedly in the middle of the manure stack outside the cow barn. I had seen a shiny object and of course wanted to examine it.

The three of us sisters shared a bedroom upstairs. My parents slept in the kitchen. In winter, when nighttime temperatures dipped to minus 30 degrees, or the 40s, or even lower, my small bed was brought down and I slept in the kitchen too, the warmest room in the house. Even so I remember my mother saying that once it had been only 7 degrees Centigrade in the morning when she got up, just a few degrees above freezing.

It was the 19 40's, the war years and beyond. Church bells would toll. Hearing them on Saturday evening on our way home across the fields, my father started reciting a poem: "…Now the bells were ringing in the Sabbath….: He liked to recite poems, and he liked to paint when he had time. He read. It was funny, when news first came that Hemingway had died, my father immediately said, "He committed suicide." It turned out to be true.

And cow bells echoed across the valley, from the enclosures near the farms. Sometimes a herd would break out of its confinement for a taste of freedom for a while. That created a minor panic each time in the household. Everyone had to take part to rein them in. You had to run, yell, whip the cows if you could.

I think back on those first eleven years with great appreciation. Not everyone saw it the same way. My oldest sister decided later that we had been taken advantage of as more or less illegal child labor. To me that was ridiculous and infuriating to hear. My other sister just hates cows in general and anything else that has to do with farms and farm work. But she doesn't apply today's standards and sensibilities to how it was then.

Everything is still there, the houses, the barns, the forest and the mountain. And yet, time has imperceptibly altered the picture. One no longer hears the lowing and the cow bells in the evening from cows anxious to get back into their barn to rest. The ground itself has moved, literally, because up north it still rises every year and in 60 years or more it has risen almost a meter. The brook which we couldn't jump over is now a narrow stream, straining to survive. I see it all from the graveyard when I visit. Something intangible is bound up to that landscape, just buried under the surface and accessible only through memory now.

Prayer for My Father

BY ERIC BARR

After the death of a parent, Jewish tradition commands the children of the deceased to go to the Synagogue every day, for 11 months to say the prayer for the dead. After my father died. I went to one Saturday service, but the rituals and language felt so alien that I never went back.

The time in that stucco Palm Springs temple left me feeling totally disconnected from my father and my heritage. On my way home I drove by a desert swap meet that my father had visited many years ago and talked about until the day he died.

I parked in the sandy lot and went looking for a particular vendor. My father had bought a knock-off Rolex from the Watch-Man and when the minute hand dropped off a few weeks later he went back and the man gave him a new replacement for free He wore his "Rolax" with pride and enjoyed showing it to friends, particularly during harsh Detroit winters, when he could tell how he bought it on a sunny and hot January morning from a man in the desert, at a steal of a price.

I found the Watch-Man, although it was his son who was now selling the "Rolax's," and bought one for myself. Then I found my father's favorite hot dog vendor and got a hot dog and lemonade, his favorite desert meal.

Sitting in the sun with my lunch, I said my own little prayer for my father. And for the first time that day, in a world without Gods or Monsters, I finally understood the prayer I was saying and why I was saying it.

The Unbearable: A Eulogy for the Daughter of My Best Friend

BY KAREN BRADFORD

Alice and I have known each other since high school, more than 55 years. When Clint and I married, which we will celebrate 35 years in one week, we said children were welcome at our ceremony. Alice and Joel brought Michelle, the most darling blondie four-year-old in a blue pinafore with long legs in white tights.

I think of Michelle when I hear the melancholy in Tevye's voice when he sings, "Is this this little girl I carried?" I'm sure Joel must have danced with his wife at our wedding, but it's little Michelle dangling in his arms that I remember. Alice told me how, for weeks later as Mrs. Spergel, Alice's mom, drove the grandchildren around Anaheim, Michelle insisted on playing "bride and groom" in the back seat with Aaron to amuse herself with this new game concept.

People talk about square pegs in round holes, but Michelle was not even that: She was ether … she was vapor, like morning mist on a tree-covered hillside that is colored by ever-changing autumn leaves, transient before the winter snows. She was a loving, accepting, generous smile who saw good in everyone and gave her heart willingly. She was all heart. She was a will o' the wisp creative being who couldn't be classified or defined or left exposed to life's harsh realities because of the fragility of her marvelous and loving soul.

Our world needs more Michelles. Our world needs the kindness that she was willing to give to anyone, as Rabbi Harold Kushner wrote in "When Bad Things Happen to Good People," not because of who they are or what they could do for her, but for who she was … and Michelle was all heart. I am grateful the world gave her to us for what time we had.

May her memory be a blessing.

The Moment When Everything Changes

by Karen Bradford

Would we even recognize when everything changed?
Is life like that?
We hope for drama, as W.H. Auden said:
Even that life may end with a bang, rather than a whimper.
We look for the "big finish."
We hope for joy.
Epiphanies!
We wish to be touched by transformation.
Not to become gods,
Nor to ascend into heaven, borne on the wings of angels.
But at least a release from the grinding, boring, vicissitudes of life.
That one made a difference:
That one had meaning.
One loved and had love.
One was remarkable.
I am. *We* are.

Old Older

by Mary Briggs

If you see me stumbling
It's not because I'm drunk
It's because I'm older, old
My memory may fail me
But not my tongue
It seems like only yesterday
That I was young, spirited, foolish
Full of daring and adventures
Now I'm no longer young
But I'm still foolish
Where have the years gone by
To oblivion
There are only memories now
Of the years gone by

The Sad Flower Pot

BY PATTY BROWN

I am a medium size terracotta flowerpot that graces the patio. My other owner decided that I would be used to hide the can filled with concrete with the O ring that they used to hold the sunscreen from blowing around when the screen was pulled down. That never made me very happy as that wasn't my purpose in life. I was made to adorn the patio with flowers, a small shrub, or a small tree. When my new owner came to live in this house, she recognized that I wasn't meant to be an anchor but to sport something of beauty. She put some rocks in the bottom and filled me with potting soil. Then she planted a gorgeous red hibiscus. I proudly showed off the beautiful flowers and continually produced more beautiful flowers. She added some petunias at the base of my trunk and when they died off, she changed to snapdragons. Then the beautiful hibiscus unexpectedly died, and I was sad as was my owner. Because she was busy doing other things and it kept raining, she didn't go buy any new flowers to fill my space. Then one day there started to be new life exploding. The snapdragons came back to life and continued to grow to fill my space with their cream and yellow flowers and to add a touch of color, there's a lone petunia making its presence known. I'm happy now that I can show off some beauty and fulfill my purpose in life. I hope that when the current flowers finally die off my owner will quickly go buy new flowers to fill my space so I can continue to bring beauty to the patio space.

Hand Lotion

BY PATTY BROWN

As the beautiful bottle sits on the nightstand with seemingly nothing to do. It can't cook, clean, do laundry, or help with any household chores, but sits there waiting for its moment of service. It is a beautiful dark blue bottle with gorgeous flowers, adorned with white writing stating the name, Moon Light Path. Claiming it has 24-hour moisture with Ultra Shea body cream and sports 8 ounces. As the lady of the house is ready to slip into bed with freshly washed hands, it's time for the beautiful bottle to shine and lovingly dispense a small amount of the rich cream to soften the lady's hands as she sleeps. Once this bottle is used and empty, it will be replaced with another bottle that will take its place in life to fulfill its mission. So goes the life cycle of the pretty bottles that adorn the nightstand of this house.

Bob

by Stephanie Bruce

For the past 6 spring/summers I have had a vegetable garden. It sits in my front yard and part of my driveway. It has produced and been delightful every year...except this year.

Well, Spring sprung and I planted lettuce and sugar snap peas in my garden box in the upper driveway area. Down below I happily planted watermelon seeds. Put in a cherry tomato, cucumber plants and golden zucchini. Bush beans went in next.

My daughter gave me 2 galvanized planters this year. 2X2x4. They were planted with beets and collard greens. Also, in pots went French tarragon, basil, and a blue berry bush.

So life began in my garden. As the watermelon shoots came up a couple of critters, with long floppy ears, hopped across the ½ acre lot and had a nighttime feast on them. I found the hole in the fence and blocked it. I almost had some moon and stars watermelon. Oh well I have plenty of other veggies, well not quite.

Then the underground tunneling thief came. I never had problems with the little brown buck toothed critters before this year. I have a name for him. It begins with a B and has 2 syllables. But I will remain a lady and just call him Bob.

Bob tunneled across my ½ acre. Under 5 feet of pavers. Under a small cement wall and systematically took out my garden, one plant at a time. Bob you little...BOB.

First, he took down my 2-foot-tall cucumber bush that was blooming with baby cucumbers all over it OH NO...I really miss my neighbor's big cat Pinky. He got the gophers every year. But this year he disappeared. Hey, maybe Bob took him out.

Next, he tunneled under another small wall with a wrought iron fence. I had enjoyed snap peas and green lettuce out of this wooden box for a month, before the wrath of Bob. Now beautiful squash plants were coming on and blooming, big orange blooms.

He took that box down in less than 3 days. Then he happily went back down to my garden below. By this time, I had been enjoying golden zucchini and cherry tomatoes. He went through my bush beans plants, pulling them down under ground. I quickly picked my zucchini and made pineapple zucchini bread for next winter. Then Bob took down my huge zucchini plant. Now most of my garden is bare thanks to Bob. We have cherry tomatoes. I guess BOB doesn't like them. At first, I was sad. But it's hot right now and I have a plan for next year and how to fix my garden. It's going to be a lot of work, but I can do it. The wonders of chicken wire and raised garden beds.

So, here is my story of my garden of 2024 and the story of BOB.

Oh, wait there he is in my front yard, I think he's waving at me. Oh Bob, you little...BOB.

Marco

by Georgette Geppert Buckley

Spring green entrances
>Sparkling turquoise to lavender shimmers
>Mes-mer-iz-es

Slipping on the rocky trail
>Towards the cliff and lake below
>My white knight rescues me

Sweet earthy air revives
>California Lavender scented
>San Marco's aromatic masterpiece

Unbottled Message

by Georgette Geppert Buckley

Breathe in the air
Feel the moisture
Along the shore

Listen
To the waves
Never Ending Love

Always coming back
Never ending Love
Always coming back

Let it surround you
He is with you
Always

Snickerdoodles: The Story

BY BRIDGETTE CALLAHAN

"[A]lways try everything even if it turns out to be a dud. We learn by doing." —Laurie Colwin

My snickerdoodles story begins on a school bus, riding to and from high school marching band competitions in 1981. We were allowed to eat on the bus, and the Davenport sisters, who were a year apart, often brought treats to share with their bandmates. I remember the rum balls and the snickerdoodles—maybe because I had never tried either, or maybe because rum balls sounded risqué to my fifteen-year-old self (are kids allowed to eat those? I remember thinking) and the name "snickerdoodle" sounded made up. I wanted to like the rum balls—which meant consuming rum (or at least something rum-flavored) on the school bus!—but I didn't like the liquor taste. While I was perplexed by the word "snickerdoodle," I loved the taste of those cookies, silly name and all.

The Davenports had family in Alabama (we often pestered the younger sister to say "Alabama" in her rendition of a southern accent), so I had always assumed that snickerdoodles were a southern thing. But I've learned that this cookie more likely originated in New England. My *Pillsbury Kitchens' Cookbook* describes a snickerdoodle as a "Tender sugar cookie with a cinnamon-sugar topping." The Betty Crocker website takes a different angle, pointing out that "classic" snickerdoodles "are often put in the same camp as sugar cookies, but the two are more like cookie cousins vs. siblings." I see Betty Crocker's point, but no matter what you call these cookies or which "camp" you place them in, as soon as my friends handed me a crackly, cinnamon-sugar-crusted snickerdoodle, I was ready to try something new.

I liked snickerdoodles so much that after I married and had a family, I made them for my four daughters. My kids grew up knowing the name "snickerdoodle," which may or may not be of Germanic origin. As mentioned on Martha Stewart's website, " 'New England cooks had a penchant for giving odd names to their dishes—apparently for no other reason than the fun of saying them.' " It's also possible that these cookies originated in Amish or Mennonite communities, and I note that there is a Mennonite group in Alabama.

My own snickerdoodle recipe is typed and stored in a binder of favorite family recipes. I recently searched my cookbook collection, trying to trace my recipe's origin, but all I found were a few recipes that don't use shortening, as mine does, and a recipe in a 1983 pocket-sized cookbook entitled *Cookie Time: Favorite Recipes Old and New*. Scrawled at the top of the recipe, my handwritten notes declare, "Bad" in pencil and "No—yuck" in pen, perhaps to ensure that I would never make that recipe again. The offending recipe contains nutmeg, walnuts, and coconut (yes, coconut!), whereas most snickerdoodle recipes are simpler, including the one I settled on for my family. Almost all snickerdoodles contain cream of tartar, which helps them rise and gives them a tangy flavor and a chewy texture.

Snickerdoodles became a tradition in my household—a favorite at Christmas—with my children and grandchildren. I've been making them with my oldest granddaughter, Maddi, since she was a little girl. Maddi is allergic to milk, so what's especially great about these cookies is that using shortening means they're dairy free. Plus, shortening tends to produce cookies that look as good as they taste.

If you decide to make snickerdoodles, I recommend opening your windows to let your neighbors enjoy the aroma of baking cookies and cinnamon (I love to be the source of a sweet scent wafting into the neighborhood). Food plays a fundamental role in our lives, and with or without a memorable name, homemade cookies can create both stories and memories.

As I always said to my girls, "Families that eat together, keep together." Stories matter. And stories worth sharing often unfold during family meals and celebrations. So I encourage you to break bread together anytime you can, and don't forget to serve snickerdoodles for dessert!

Snickerdoodles

1 cup shortening or softened margarine

1 ½ cups sugar

2 eggs

2 ½ cups flour

2 tsp. cream of tartar

1 tsp. baking soda

½ tsp. salt

2 tsp. cinnamon + ¼ cup sugar

Preheat oven to 350*

In large bowl, cream shortening (or margarine) and sugar; beat in eggs. In smaller bowl, stir or whisk together flour, cream of tartar, baking soda, and salt; stir into creamed mixture. Cover and refrigerate one hour (if pressed for time, you can skip this step; however, the cookies may spread too much and run together!).

Form dough into walnut-sized balls and roll in a cinnamon-sugar mixture—use half cinnamon, half sugar for an intense cinnamon taste. Or if you're not into cinnamon and/or the cookies are for a holiday, roll the dough balls in colored sugar.

Place dough balls about two inches apart on *un*greased baking sheets. Bake at 350* for 9-12 minutes, until tops are cracking (for softer cookies, bake 9-10 minutes). Transfer cookies to wire racks to cool. (Makes 4 dozen.)

Helpful hints: Snickerdoodles are best when served *before* dinner and accompanied by a story—always share your cookies and your stories. You might just create some delicious memories.

End Notes

Laurie Colwin. *Home Cooking: A Writer in the Kitchen*, Vintage Books, 1988, p. 179.

Pillsbury Kitchens' Cookbook. Pillsbury, 1979, p. 165.

"Classic Snickerdoodle Cookies." *Betty Crocker*, www.bettycrocker. com/recipes/classic-snickerdoodle-cookies/7ffc92a9-d847-4869-9ecb-99de3b751b14.

Ellen Morrissey. "What Is a Snickerdoodle, and What Makes This Classic American Cookie So Irresistible?" *Martha Stewart*, 26 June 2020, www.marthastewart.com/7839907/snickerdoodle-cookie-explained.

Lorrie DeRose. *Cookie Time: Favorite Recipes Old and New*. Guide Books, 1983, p. 33.

Imagine
by Darcel Cannady

As soon as i
patted her haunches
she launches
into a prance
that created a dance
of magic
and mystery
and off we went
to travel through
history
i could hardly
hold her reigns
as we ascended
to the sky
to reign
above the fray
of fractured times
to rain down
seeds of a new dawn
of open minds
peaceful hearts
and full bellies
laughter
and smiles
all the while
to the sounds
of sweet soul music
we were riding
a wild whirl wind
trying to create
a world

where freedom
reigned supreme
i found myself
saying
"whoa girl
not too fast
i want to
let this feeling last
for as long
as the sun shines
and the waters flow."

if i could, i would

by Darcel Cannady

if i could, i would
begin
and end
each day
with a prayer
"a day hemmed
in prayer
is less likely
to unravel"
if i could, i would
hold on to
threads of hope
weaving my
basket of grace
fill it with
love
and scatter
it like
parade confetti
where it can
settle into
the cracks
and crevices
of discord
transforming
dreams
and
granting
wishes
if i could, i would
tap into

the light
that resides
in each of us
creating
a synergistic
glow that can
only be seen
by the torch bearers
of tomorrow
those who
savor
the leaf light
bottling the
rays
of compassion
to release
on the gloom
that threatens
to consume us
if i could, i would
devise a plan
to remind man
that hu-man-i-ty
includes
us
all

The Wind Phone

BY ELLEN DAVIDSON CANTOR

"Because my thoughts couldn't be relayed over a regular phone line, I wanted them to be carried on the wind." Itaru Sasaki, founder of The Wind Phone

I yearn to talk to you. I miss our daily chats. Now, instead of keeping my words inside of me, I speak out loud, telling you my ups and downs, remembering how we used to share our life.

I call you on The Wind Phone.

Untethered to telephone poles or fiber optics, The Wind Phone allows me to speak to you once again.

I call you on The Wind Phone

I describe joyous and heartbroken events, missed celebrations, family stories of birth and death, tales of sadness and grief that live deep within me. I whisper "I Love You."

I call you on The Wind Phone.

I share daily happenings at home such as the leaky pool that cost thousands to repair, the California native garden planted to save water, the graceful teak bench where I watch your favorite birds drink at the birdbath.

I call you on The Wind Phone.

I tell you about our four grandsons: Anthony's 16th birthday celebration with a cake shaped like a baseball, Zach's recovery from ACL, MCL and meniscus surgery, Jacob's girlfriend and their matching cowboy hats; Max's new found strength pinning his opponents in wrestling.

I call you on The Wind Phone.

I relay messages about everyday occurrences: watching Jeopardy the way we did nightly, checking out the news with David Muir, writing poetry to guide me through my grief journey, selling one of my multiple image photographs, daily trips to radiation for my skin cancer, struggling with a purple cast on my broken right wrist that leaves me helpless, loneliness when I go to bed.

I call you on The Wind Phone.

Now, when I tell you an anecdote or share a secret, I know you will hear me.

Words Before Boot Hill

by Alben J. Chamberlain

I'm sorry that I can't leave
a fortune for my posterity.
I didn't spend the years of my life
diligently seeking after prosperity.

I'm sorry I never achieved even
fifteen minutes of adulation and fame.
I can only hope that my choices and
actions have left you a good name.

Nobody will ever remember all
the bills and taxes that I paid.
I certainly hope they'll forgive
all the mistakes that I made.

I hope you'll gain something from
all the lessons that I've learned.
At least you won't need to worry
about all the bridges that I've burned.

I hope that, with my written words,
some life lessons will remain.
I sure as hell won't be earning
literary accolades or acclaim.

I hope you'll remember my constant
love of reading, study, and learning.
In paradise, knowledge and wisdom are more
vital than the fortunes that we now are earning.

I hope you'll forgive me for all the
expressions of love that I've left unsaid.
I know it will be too late when the call
comes that all we humans dread.

I hope you don't waste the time that I
have by my poor choices and indecision.
The days of this life pass like a mirage
or a passing rainbow-hued vision.

I know now that family and relationships
are the greatest treasures you can find.
All this world's fortunes, fame, and
properties will, at death, be left behind.

Too soon, I'll be up on boot hill where
the dry and dusty winds blow.
Put my rocks around that lonely
mound to put on a good show.

Plant some poppies or daisies there
to brighten up the fleeting day.
They're a reminder that even nature's
greatest beauty won't forever stay.

Putting a bird feeder on that hill
might be worth your while.
When you drop by for a visit,
they might bring you a smile.

Keep all my poems and stories handy
to serve as my final epigraph.
You never know when you'll be
in need of a good, long laugh.

Just know that when my days
here on this earth are through;
my greatest pleasure and joy
was spending them with you.

Moon

by Natalie Michele Champion

A bright moon shining
A white-plumed bird flying in
The crisp nighttime sky

Moonlight Shimmers
BY NATALIE MICHELE CHAMPION

Moonlight shimmers on our passion-stricken faces,
As we lay together,
Enveloped in each other's warmth,
Our bodies,
Our souls one with each other,
In time with the rhythm of our love-making,
Our hearts pulsing with love for each other,
Thankful for this blessed night together.

Peggy O' Brian
by Richard Champion

Peggy played with dolls. She invited her stuffed animals to tea parties and served them pretend tea. I thought she was off the edge, although I did not know that phrase at six years old.

My mother said, "Peggy wants to marry you". Confused, I answered, "Girls get married. Boys don't."

My mother was about to set me straight, but a motorcycle roared down our street. After the dogs had chased the motorcycle out of our neighborhood, she enlightened me. "Your father and I are married." Confused, I put my objection on hold.

Peggy's grandma lived in a stone house that had been a ranch house and after that a movie star's hideaway. The house was surrounded by trees, thick with leaves, that shaded the yard. There was a fountain in the yard. It was cool there always. From our house through the screen door and across the street we saw along a driveway that went to the back of grandma's house. My mom said, "Come see what Peggy is doing now."

Later, in the third grade, Sister Rose Eileen bravely tried to teach us Latin. Her patience gave out. Later still, my mother decided that she wanted me to help the Priest at mass. She sent me to Jimmy to learn Latin. He was already an altar boy. I asked him, "What do the words mean?" He answered, "It doesn't matter. You just say them." I washed out of altar boy training. Later still, when the Church was thinking that maybe God could understand us better in English than in broken Latin, essays began to appear in Catholic magazines. My mother was dismissive.

"Just seminarians too lazy to learn Latin."

A motorcycle pack roared by. Dogs howled and chased after, barking.

When Peace returned, my mother said, "Peggy and Danny and Robin are saying mass."

At Saint Anthony's school, I saw Sisters and Priests, so I thought boys could grow up to be Priests and girls could grow up to be Sisters. But here was Peggy, with a towel wrapped around her shoulders, holding up a pretend Host. Peggy had been paying attention.

Peggy's little brother, Danny, was her altar boy. I thought that only boys could be with the Priest at the altar. But Peggie's cousin, Robin, was with her, too. Much later, Holy Mother Church made a concession. Both boys and the girls could help the Priest at mass, but differently. Boys would do what they had always done: pour water and wine. Girls would carry candles when the Priest came into church and when he read the Gospel. It was just like boys and girls playing with different toys: Girls with dolls and boys with airplanes. But the girls kept insisting that they could do whatever boys could do.

Cura personales is Latin for care of the person. It can be applied to mitigate damage from overzealous application of rules. One day the grandfatherly Priest was assisted at mass by brother and sister altar servers. At water and wine time the brother spaced out. His sister was about to step in, but the Priest waved her away. She was crestfallen. Like a good grandfather, the Priest thought of her well being first. He motioned her to pour the water and wine. Big smile.

Since that time the gender requirement for that job has been removed.

My family lost contact with Peggy's family when we moved to follow my Father's job. Long after, she contacted my mother asking about godparents.

Now I live in San Francisco's Bayview District, but still with motorcycles who run in packs and rear up, back wheels only, like stallions. With no dogs to chase them off, I attempt peaceful accommodation. They even follow me to the Haight Ashbury.

Maria organized a retreat at Saint Vincent's School for bad

boys, her husband's *Alma Mater*. We crossed the Golden Gate Bridge and entered the Rainbow Tunnel. On the other side we saw, at the back of a large pasture, buildings that suggested a mission or religious community.

Mary Ann had a basket with a bottle of wine and a baguette peeking from under what appeared to be a picnic blanket. "We're going to do something with Maria," she said. I envisioned a picnic in the shade of an oak tree. Perhaps there were olives, cheese, salami, and chocolate in the basket. Maria appeared with keys. But we didn't go to the oak tree. Maria led us into the chapel announcing that we were going to say some prayers.

Maria and Mary Ann giggled as they spread the picnic blanket over the altar. Wine and water followed, as well as the chalice-a large wine glass. Maria spoke the opening words. My contribution was reading from scripture. Maria blessed the baguette, broke it, and gave out communion.

The mass is not a mechanical ritual. It is a personal expression of the faith of the presider as well as a personal invitation to share that faith. Men and women are complementary. Each gender touches something in the heart that the other does not.

Maria could have been legal if, rather than a mass, she had led a communion service-reserved for when a priest is absent or unavailable. This is a half-step. The presider is not supposed to say, "Go the Mass is ended," because it could not be an official Mass. Nor can the presider pronounce the words of Consecration. That has to be done off line by an officially ordained man, with the hosts being later taken to the communion service.

I have a bottom line on this and it's about getting real. Women want to hold up half of the sky. Let them do it.

Never Say Never

by Sylvia Clarke

As we are growing up, my sister Elvina and I seem to have very different ideas about what we will do after we finish high school.

"Maybe I'll take a short course in something and get a job," Elvina muses, "or get married." I, on the other hand, tell myself— if not others—that I will not marry until I finish college. Probably the major influence in this line of thought is my father.

I turn five the autumn Dad and Mom pull up stakes in Montana and move to eastern Washington where Daddy starts his theology degree at Walla Walla College. By the time he graduates in 1951, I know that I will go to college when I grow up—no question.

Fortunately for me, before I finish high school at Cedar Lake Academy in Michigan, Mother's brother, Uncle Elvin, starts a savings account for me that includes the $100 that I need as an entrance fee at Andrews University in southwestern Michigan. After working in the kitchen at Camp AuSable all summer, I head to college for the next chapter in my life: more education!

At the beginning of my second year of college, something new and interesting enters my life. Among the workers gathered at the custodial window to be assigned work, a different accent, red hair, and glasses catch my attention. Who is he and where does he come from?

I not only find out but begin spending time with him and— you guessed it—end up marrying Wilton before I finish college— but after he does!

My sister? Well, Elvina spends a year teaching first grade after she earns her BA degree and before she marries Deane Wolcott. One never knows what the future will bring, so the injunction to never say never is meant to keep us flexible and ready to consider new possibilities. After all, I don't want to keep a good man waiting, or I might lose him!

Christmas Hike in Madagascar 2015

by Wil Clarke

It was Christmas Day, 2015. Sylvia and I had volunteered to teach English for a semester at Zurcher Adventist University (UAZ) in Madagascar. Gideon and Pam Petersen were instrumental in getting us to join their faculty temporarily. They invited us to go up a nearby mountain range and see a mountain lake and waterfalls. Being in the southern hemisphere, it was early summer and the weather was beautiful.

We hiked across the main north-south highway of the country and down past a mud brick church that the UAZ students had constructed a few years previously. The footpath led down through a pine forest that had been slashed to produce amber/gum. Then down to a narrow raging torrent of a river that was spanned by about four slippery, debarked logs. Imagine my terror and pride as I watched Sylvia make it across the torrent without slipping. The east side of the valley was carved up into endless rice paddies. Each paddy was separated from its adjacent paddy by a mud wall that rice farmers kept intact by a spade. We got to the far side of the valley and started up along the edges of the terraced paddies.

We climbed steeper and steeper hills, wending our way through a village and between burial structures, that house the sacred ancestors of this animist society. Then higher up the mountain side. Finally, we found a fairly steep meadow and sat down while Pam spread out a delicious picnic lunch and we sat and surveyed the valley, with the university on the far side. It was green and heavily terraced.

As we watched we saw a tropical storm come up on the university. It was raining hard and sported a beautiful rainbow. It crept inexorably toward the pine forest, and the little church. While it slid like a snail with a great grey shell on its back, masking everything it passed over, we began to discuss our predicament. Should we go on up to the promised lake, or head home? Finally we packed up our few belongings and as the initial great drops started pelting us we started back down the path towards home.

The hard red clay of the footpath quickly turned in very sticky clay, and our feet slid at every step. We didn't run—it was too slick and where would we run to, anyway? The sky grew very dark and was punctuated by flashes of lightning and menacing thunder. Before we had gone a hundred yards, we were soaked to the skin. The rain was warm and very wet. We slipped and slid back down the terraces. Everyone of us fell at one point or another and was covered with the Red Island mud. The pelting downpour helped wash some of the mud from our clothes and bodies. We couldn't see very far and would have been totally lost, had we not had a university student with us who knew the way and which paddies to go around on the left of and which to the right.

Then we got back to the three logs. We could hear the surge of the torrent before we got there. Under this cloudburst, the swollen flood rushed angrily by. The logs were still above the water, but even more slippery now than when we had crossed earlier that day. With a silent prayer for protection, we crept carefully back across. To slip into the water meant sudden death. As we passed the little church, the tropical storm began to subside. And by the time we crossed the north-south highway it had pretty much stopped. We sloshed the half-mile or so from the highway to our home. We stood on the front porch and stripped to our skin, so we didn't bring the muck and mud into the house.

We just love the adventures we have as we travel.

Proof I Had a Father

by James Coats

Rest now you rogue, for the day is won
Spirit forced to cross the enemies' line
The battle fiercely fought, is finally done

What is left but memories for a son
I had you with me though you were not mine
Rest now, you rogue, for the day is won

Evening shadow could never eclipse your run
Inferno inside dimmed to embers over time
The battle fiercely fought, is finally done

Seasons measure the distance we've come
My mind polishes early moments to a shine
Rest now you rogue, for the day is won

Beauty escapes a body left numb
Grief stabs sudden, as a brutal crime
The battle fiercely fought, is finally done

Your absence of breath weighs a ton
How soon ash is blown too far to find
Rest now you rogue for the day, is won
The battle, fiercely fought, is finally done

Returning to the Sea

BY JAMES COATS

Poetry is like water.
It's inside everyone,
even the people that don't believe
they need a thirst quenched,
even they cannot live without hydration.
Poetry is inside every tiny cell of our body
moving and shifting as oceans over time.

Like you I am born from water
precious liquid streaming in my blood
like rivers that refuse to be held back
like waterfalls not afraid to leap from cliffs
and make a splash.
Like you I've known of still lakes
filled by dew, lost in forbidden forest,
seeking out the serenity of peaceful sunlight.

Like water I have no allegiance to place.
I go where the wind carries me.
I land where the ground calls my name,
to feed any nation, every people
with life,
with love,
with the question only answered by the deepest parts
of our own understanding.

Like you I have traveled
a great distance to be here.
Still unraveling each new state of my being
still holding together a hope
even after hurt has hurricane to my world

and what was up is now upside down
and the places that were once home,
today feels totally foreign.

I still find my way into everything.
Every flower-song pulsing by a riverbed.
Every tear leaking from an innocent child's eyes.
Every word stuck in the silk of your saliva.
I am the part of you that stays
And the part that returns to the sea.

Like you,
I love and wish to be loved
and I am here with you now.
Open.
Waiting for you to love me back
however long that takes.

AA Batteries

by Elinor Cohen

Now where are those interview tapes? I know I saw them during the Great Covid Cleanup of 2020. In a box in the bedroom closet? Bingo. Now, um, where can I find a tape player? A machine that plays a tape? A standard plastic cassette tape? Found, right here, one of those silver Sony Walkman-sized voice recording devices that made me feel like a journalist the minute I picked it up. I bet you need a charge, you little battery-powered bastard. Nope, still kicking. Thanks Energizer, your Bunny does keep going and going.

This little gadget is so convenient to use! Said no one at all in the last two decades. Pro: it fits nicely in the palm of my hand. Con: the pop-up buttons were designed to be operated by a kindergartener. How are my fashionably fat fingers going to manipulate these minuscule metal tabs? Seriously, have my fingers doubled in size since I sat across from my father all those years ago, asking him questions about the fascinating twists his life had taken, making sure to position the recorder an even distance away from each of us to achieve the ultimate in consistent sound (but I remember that somehow my mother's cheeky comments made from the far-away kitchen were also perfectly audible). Was that right before they split up? Before they declared war on marriage and each other?

I press PLAY and hear myself say "Aba Interview, Tape One" (Aba is what I call him, it's Hebrew for Father). Then an annoying series of rhythmic clicks as I got the tape recorder situated on the table, and then Aba spoke. "My name is Coco, because I was born Jacques Charles, which was too long to call me when we had lunch." I gasped, took a deep loud heavy breath in and held it. I didn't mean to, but this was the first time I heard his voice since he died four years ago. He continued from the tape: "We were seven brothers and sisters, to call everybody by their full names would have taken too much time, and the food would be cold. So we all had nicknames." I press STOP.

Whoa, okay, maybe I'm not ready for this. I look behind me for a place to sit down and realize I'm already sitting. I thought enough time had passed for me to listen to these tapes without bawling like a baby. Or is it sobbing like a sissy? What is it I'm doing now? Hyperventilating like a hyena? It's been almost four years to the day since the Chevra Kadisha holy burial society sent a fleet of rabbis-in-training to dig a proper Hebrew hole and lift my papa's soul high into the heavens while lowering his old bones deep into the ground. I wrote his obituary, where I described him as a rock drummer, a soccer player, hotel manager, army lieutenant, limo driver, aspiring stage actor, impassioned reader, dedicated movie goer, record collector, thrift shop supporter, macho fashionista, charming hustler, and incurable serial flirt who loved a good pedicure and always saw the best in people. I remember writing it, editing and cutting for content, and discarding descriptions like "amateur magician" and "teller of Dad Jokes" because the newspaper charged for the obituary by the line. I also remember feeling immensely guilty for thinking about the money, but convinced myself that he wasn't actually that great of a teller of jokes, so I could justify leaving it out for a more honorable reason.

So maybe I need to ease into this whole thing more slowly. Find a new approach. A radically different approach. What if I start by collecting some background information about Morocco, where my dad was born. A little harmless research, low-level emotion, no tears. Didn't I just get an email last month from my college alumni association about a group trip to Morocco? Lemme check. Scrolling, scrolling, there. Explore the vibrant and alluring wonders of Morocco with Inspired Expeditions, UC Santa Cruz's travel program for alumni and friends. Okay, I'm listening, details please.

"The Moroccan journey begins exploring Casablanca with its burgeoning arts scene, and Rabat, the country's capital and diplomatic center. Bask in the imperial city of Meknes and the ancient Roman settlement of Volubilis. Prepare your camera for the picturesque seaside town of Essaouira, and in Marrakesh, an ancient trading center, spend time discovering the city's proud traditional artisanship. End the program by exploring villages located deep in the High Atlas mountains and learning about the unique ways of life of Morocco's native peoples, the Berbers."

Hell yeah, I'm in. When are we going? October? Perfect, I'll clear my pretend schedule. How much does this cost? So much money that the email doesn't even dare tell me how much money. I'll dip into my pretend savings account. And pretend renew my passport. It's all pretend good.

But what else can I learn about my ancestral lands? Let's take it to Google. All the readily available info, the usual suspects, Capital: Rabat. King: Mohamed VI. Language: Arabic. Currency: Dirham. Boring stuff, what else you got? Where are the meaningful statistics? Oh here we go. Life Expectancy at Birth: 71 years. Adult Literacy Rate: 56%. Infant Mortality Rate: 32 per 1,000 live births. Hmmm. In the US, the infant mortality rate is 6 per 1,000 live births. Just sayin'. So what are other people asking Google? Ahem, from *People also ask*: Can I drink alcohol in Morocco? Are you allowed to kiss in public? Can unmarried couples live together? [followed immediately by] How many wives can you have? (the answer is "up to four" if you're curious). Can women own property? What do Moroccans eat for breakfast? Why do they eat with their hands? How much is a Coke? How do you say hi? How do you say shut up? Is Morocco better than India? <sigh>. People are so interesting.

It's been almost a whole day. Sixteen hours have passed. I tell myself I'm ready to listen to a little bit more of the tape. I reheat my coffee and settle into my chair. I press PLAY and there he is again, talking in that velvet voice. "My grandfather Jacob worked in a hardware store all his life because he was big and strong. I remember him being so tall because I was so little, he must have been the same size I am today." Here I go, crying like a crazy person again. But I don't pause, I let him keep going. "One day he saw a woman that was so beautiful, he fell in love with her right away. So he went tooo sseeee tthhheee moootttherrr oofff tthh-heee ggggirrrlllll…" Distorted trailing off sound, then silence. Dead battery. I rattle the device around a little, trying to knock some juice back in. Shake shake shake. I smack it from one hand to another. Nothing. Eh. Fuck you, Energizer, I should've gone with Duracell. Apparently, you can't top the copper top.

To be continued after I go buy a pack of AA's at the drugstore.

Abuelita Chuchi

by Hilda Cruz
— a blues poem

My thoughts run to our last words, our last embrace.
That I could say I love you one more time,
That I could thank you for the gift of life,
That I could hold you in a long, tight embrace.

Our next encounter I see you, I seek your warmth,
yet it's not there. You've gone to eternal rest.
To a great reunion, where passed loved ones dwell.
To a beautiful place where all is well.

I feel your presence but there is
no warm embrace, no goodbye kiss.
Among mine, I see your descent to the earth,
flowers thrown your way, my life an abyss.

Matriarch on my father's side.
The trunk of my ancestral tree; strong, abundant,
embracing, nurturing, ever loving, even from the afterlife.
Te honro, te amo Abuelita Chuchi.

Pansies (pensamientos) Abuelita Virginia

BY HILDA CRUZ

—an epistolary poem

I see a pansy and think of you,
watering the flowerbeds you loved,
heart shape, velvety,
violet, yellow, and hues of blue.

In a pansy I see you
small and delicate,
velvety to my touch.

Saturday mornings spent outside.
Tilling the soil and watering plants.
Surrounded by beautiful blossoms
tended with pride.

So many things bring you to mind,
like the Canaries you so loved,
and the Christmas ornament with bird songs, that
is now mine.

Church holiday preparations and practices
kept us busy and involved.
This way you taught us and passed on
your faith of a Higher Being that created us all.

I hope you are proud of what I have tended and grown.
A garden of nine children and fourteen precious retoños so far.
Like your garden, they have spread, some live here
others abroad, ever growing, blossoming and healing the land.

In the beauty of my children and my retoños, I see you;
Tilling the soil and watering plants,
Surrounded by beautiful blossoms
tended with pride.

Abuelita Virginia, in my pensamientos you always are.

Learning to Drive
BY CHUCK DOOLITTLE

Reaching the age of fifteen thrilled my parents beyond measure. I'd been a teenager for a few years but now it was approaching what I know they'd anticipated anxiously, their youngest starting to drive. Not only was I a dutiful boy, take my word for that, but I was trustworthy and the apple of their eyes, trust me on that one too. They couldn't wait. The time had arrived for me to sit behind their 3500 lb. investment with many lives completely in my hands. They'd never been happier. My dad was so overjoyed that he was gentlemanly enough to hand over the entire job of training me to my mom. And I'd never quite seen the look on my mom's face upon hearing this news, but it must have been none other than sheer joy.

Our green, 1955 Chevrolet Bel Air station wagon was the means with which I'd be learning the ropes. It wasn't brand new, but it could have been a Lamborghini for all I was concerned. I was already thinking of it as mine. Mom thought we should get a head start on the training, or maybe that was me. Either way, she preferred the empty high school parking lot on a weekend for our first few ventures. I wouldn't leave her alone until we finally left the house. I noticed my mom had that same look on her face. She must have been as excited as I was to start.

The high school parking lot was not that exciting to look at, but it seemed like Le Mans to me. I imagined the other cars I was racing in my Lambo. I hardly remembered my mom was in the car until I heard, "Chuckie, slow down! Watch that turn! Don't brake so hard." It was obvious she was having fun! The occasional burning rubber and the screech of the brakes just added to her enjoyment. I bet she was glad she got this job from my dad now.

The real fun began when we decided that I should learn to

drive our stick shift. That meant driving our blue fifty-nine Datsun 210 on the dirt roads of Chase Drive in Corona. Chase Drive was a popular place for kids to make out and party as well as a perfect location for a wannabe driver. The stick put the automatic to shame. Now my imagination really ran wild, remembering movies where the car chase scenes always involved revving engines and shifting gears. I'll never forget that shift pattern – H – first top left, second bottom left, third top right, fourth bottom right, and reverse bottom to the right of fourth with a push in to get it in gear. I had entered a whole, new world, and the familiar look on mom's face told me she had too. What a blast.

The rest is history. I'm quite certain I've gone on to become one of the best drivers of all time. The thirteen tickets between the ages of 16 and 24 are no sign of my ability. They simply imply that police officers are human and, accordingly, prone to mistakes. If you still have some doubts, you need to look no further than my mother. She'd be happy to tell you, slightly tongue in cheek, that teaching me to drive was the time of her life.

Feeling Small

by Reiss DuPlessis

I am well over six feet tall and, often, overweight. I never feel small. Indeed, I always feel like I'm towering over the world. There was an evening, several years ago, when I went to a local bowling alley with my staff to enjoy a nice evening of togetherness away from the office. It was going well, the staff was enjoying and I was happy I had agreed to the outing.

Suddenly, I had a very strange feeling. I felt small. I will admit, it was disconcerting. I wondered if I should leave the lanes and go outside for a breath of fresh air.

I told Deana, one of my coworkers, how I was feeling. She looked at me and giggled. I thought, this was not a laughing matter. I felt very strange and very small!

With the most taunting grin on her usually friendly face, she giggled, "Look around you, that's the Rams Football team bowing beside us!"

"There's gold in them thar hills"

by Jerry Ellingson

Many years ago, my daughter, Andrea, my grandson, Colin, and I went to Northern California for a vacation. In a little, old mining town, we stopped to pan for gold. There, we experienced a memorable vacation and learned a great life lesson. Our prospector guide began teaching that lesson by teaching us the following rules.

Steps to Proper Gold Panning

1. Get rid of rocks

2. Cull out useless sand and stones

3. Don't lose your gold

First step - Fill the pan with soil from the bottom of the creek and place the whole pan under the water. This is what the prospectors called scratching the dog's belly. You sift through sand, pull out the big rocks and throw them away.

Second step – Fill the pan with water and move the pan side to side. This separates the sand from the small pebbles and rocks. You throw them out one by one. You are working down, hopefully, to the gold at the bottom of the pan.

Third step – Dip the front of the pan just under the water and begin a swirling motion in the pan. This moves the sand around back out into the stream. The sand is lighter than the black sand and that holds the gold flakes and nuggets. These will stay at the bottom of your pan, but you need to make sure you don't accidentally throw away the gold.

After the prospector showed us the 3 steps, he left us on our own. We took soil from the big bucket that came from a spot in the stream and began repeating the steps. The rock I was sitting on was hard, real hard. After a while, my arms hurt, and my shoulders ached. I was thinking, "What are we doing here? We could have gone for a nice drive. We could have gone shopping. I could be cleaning the toilets at the hotel. Anything would be easier than this."

I looked at my daughter and said, "This is really hard work." "I know" she said. We both went back to working the pan. I was thinking to myself, "We paid $140.00 to do this. We can't just go home."

We both continued to work in silence. After a while, without even realizing it, my arms and shoulders weren't hurting, and the rock didn't seem hard. The breeze was drifting across the water, and the sunlight was dancing through the leaves. The rhythm of my body had united into the rhythm of my surroundings like a beautiful melody. Just as I looked at my daughter, she looked at me. I could tell from the look on her face that she was feeling the same thing I was feeling. She smiled and said, "This is nice." "Yes, it is." I said, and we both went back to work.

We finished panning the soil in the bucket and then the old prospector explained how the gold was washed out of the hills and into the stream. He showed us how to sluice the stream and now we had a better understanding of where the gold could be found, increasing our chances of collecting richer sand. By the end of the day, we had a little vial filled with gold flakes.

Even after the vacation was over, I was still on a "gold fever high." I get giddy thinking about that wonderful day spent in the stream, panning for gold. It isn't about finding a million-dollar nugget – I realized it is because life is like panning for gold. Yes! Life.

During our life, a bunch of dirt is dropped into our pan. There is some gold waiting to be found, but first we must dig through the bad stuff to get what we want. Each one of us is different, but what we need to work through, to get what we want, for our life goals might be a bad relationship, unfounded fears, petty jealousies, addictions, prejudices.

With the bad stuff out of the way, we can now discover the important things we want to keep in our lives. Things like fulfilling personal relationships, strong spiritual values, financial security, recreation that recreates, a rewarding job.

There is gold in "them thar hills." By using proper techniques, we can ensure that we will all discover the gold we are searching for in our lives.

I wish you all "Happy panning."

One More Reason Charlotte Regretted Not Having Daughters

by Bryan Franco

Charlotte's boys built a snowman while she cooked
her famous pineapple white chocolate
snow day flap jacks.
As the kids smothered maple cardamom coconut cream
on the jacks, she noticed a band
of fuchsia on the snow man.
She layered up in long johns, fleece sweats,
ski socks, and vinyl knee-high snow boots.
Charlotte tromped through post-blizzard snow
to discover her $250 designer cashmere scarf
on the snowman.
The water damage was irreparable
according to the dry cleaner.
After the snow melted, she handed
her eldest son a spade
to dig a grave.
She had her youngest son
play taps on a kazoo while
the middle son recited
The Lord is My Shepherd
in its entirety.
The cashmere scarf was buried in a Havanista
cedar cigar box coffin.
For posterity, her husband videotaped
the only funeral for a scarf
in modern history.
During the ceremony,
Charlotte drank from a goblet
filled with farm-fresh apple cider
she secretly wished was rum.

Bamboo Who

by Bryan Franco

Knock, knock…My name is Bamboo.
I am a rigid weed
You must clear cut several times a year.
If you plant me,
I will invade your space.
I can expand from thicket to forest
in record time.
It's not my fault that Gaia or God
or whoever created me pieced me
together with the blood and guts
that compose my being.
You can harvest my body
for your floors and furniture
and make paper, clothing, or
thousand-thread-count sheets with
the fibers you extract from my soul.
If you use me for charcoal, your
slow-smoked meats will be as sweet as
Tupelo honey and tender as a Van Morrison song.
I may not be as pretty as a Crepe Myrtle,
and yes, I multiply like rabbits
and overstay my welcome, but
you can drill holes in me, and
finally learn to play the flute
like you always wanted to.

Nora's Quilt

by Nan Friedley

she made many
some were passed on to me
mine traveled from
an Indiana farmhouse
to a stucco house in California
my favorite lays
on a guest room bed
some frayed segments
testament to years of use
and storage in a cedar chest
dating back to the early 1900's

my great grandma
saved depression era prints
from family clothing she had made
crafted a wedding ring pattern with
lavender daisy remnants
from a dress Grandma wore
red and white polka dot leftover
swatches of an uncle's shirt
cotton strips of teal leaves
cream colored backing
stretched on a wooden frame
stitched meticulously, scalloped
border trimmed in red

i was only six when Nora passed away
in those days they called it
"hardening of the arteries"
now it's called dementia
my memories of her are skewed
but she left a lasting legacy
a family history in fabric
pieced together to tell our story

Father's Day

by Nan Friedley

two days before, hospice called, end
of life was coming, at 96, Alzheimer's

has been stealing his memory for years
no longer remembered me

I remember when he set up our
swing set in the backyard

I remember the times he fixed
flat tires on my Schwinn bike

I remember he taught me
how to write a check at the kitchen table

I remember he barbecued ribs
to kick off the summer on Memorial Day

I remember when he drove Sheryl (sis)
and me to college in our station wagon

I remember when he saw his first
grandson, so pleased to finally have a boy

I remember he played piano for him
couldn't stop smiling

I love that smile
I'll remember it always

Let Me

by Ginger Galloway

sometimes you just have to let me be
who i am
broken and chipped
faded
with batteries spent
squeaks and squeals
loud
messy and oftentimes disheveled
a being full of joy that overflows onto the floor and
puddles around my feet
where laughter has no boundaries
the silliness of it all
of everything
bits of this and that
memories that awaken during
the prayer at church
being stomping mad with anger
red-hot
just-let-me-drive away from here
see you in the distance
like a stranger who couldn't care
about tantrums or
attitudes
or wrinkled blouses
walking by as if who i am
doesn't affect who you are
being an exhausted queen whose subjects
don't care that the castle
brick by brick
is falling into the moat
swallowed up by murky water

and toothless
crocodile
an orb dented and missing stones
in her hand
useless and downtrodden
because being herself is hard
and embarrassing
embarrassing when things don't go
or stay
cheeks flush
eyes bloodshot
hands that shiver
words that just will not stop
saying things
that should not be said
rules that prevent
movement into spaces
when you prevent
movement into spaces
where i just wish to exist

One Cloth

by Ginger Galloway

His laughter makes me look
over my shoulder at a
deep and resounding
HA!
A laugh at the steps that I take
pigeon footed
and stumbling
in shoes warn on the sides
He reaches
big hands toward outstretched arms
picking me up
again
I'm wrapped in laughter that between us
I understand
that He understands
words that he doesn't say
that I don't say
perfect
my legs ankles and toes that twist
knees that kiss
just like his

Hell's Kitchen
BY CAMILLE GAON

Resentment is simmering on the back burner
Hatred is boiling over in the stockpot on the front burner
Anxiety is curdling in the bain-marie on the other back burner
Stress is sizzling in the large sauté pan on the other front burner
Panic is cooking in the paella pan on the third back burner
Frustration is roasting to a golden crispness in the oven
Anger is ready to explode in the crockpot
Sadness is steaming in the soup pot on the third front burner
Stupidity is popping like popcorn in the microwave
Fear is frozen stiff in the freezer
And don't even get me started on what's in the pantry or who's
    in the deep freezer in the garage.
Anxiety is broiling in the toaster oven
Agitation is spinning out of control in the Vita Mix
Irritation is filled to the brim in the Brita water pitcher
Desperation is somewhere on the spice rack
Contempt is in the creeping grapevines on the backyard fence
Bitterness is growing deep roots in the herb garden
Hope, happiness, love and joy are in the garbage can at the curb
    in front of the house
And guilt is nowhere to be found
The result of our most recent election.

"Is This Mic On"

by Chris "The Poetic Genius" Green
— a cento

Forkfuls of family conversation slicing years of silence
None of these faces look familiar, neither does the one in the mirror
We find no secrets,
and yet how different every sentence sounds heard across the years
I don't know if there is a word for being both hungry and full
but maybe there's a song for it
They take me on a tour of their feelings
I have to come back for more
There is a magic made by melody: A spell of rest, and quiet breath, and cool
Microphone check,
Microphone check
One-two
Sources: Gye Nyame, Jorge Mendez, Terra Leigh, Dana Gioia, Dave Harris, and Elizabeth Bishop

Gloucester

BY CHRIS "THE POETIC GENIUS" GREEN

The George P. Coleman Bridge
Allows me to drive over the river my ancestors were shipped
    across
For years I've paid the toll to return
Still not equal to their toll of toiling as captives in this land
    that captivates me
Forgetting their language, names, heritage in this town I call
    my own
Their history forgotten like my place on the map
In a marred hidden gem in Virginia's crown
Gloucester, with its country-city aesthetic
Trying to grow and change and maintain its identity
A southern state not deemed southern enough,
but still holds southern sensibilities
Where yes ma'am and no sir still hold currency
A mix of vernacular here
Mostly white, mostly out of towners christened Virginians here
Black folk with beginnings here
Broken English, a language we never mastered from our
    masters
But innovated as we integrated here
Racism conquered daily the way we commune here
Gather for festivals when the daffodils bloom here
Guinea jubilee bringing bubbas and brothers together
Gloucester, where big muddy trucks and decked out cars with
    rims
Park on the same street
Where hunting jackets and peacoats can fashion together
In this American fabric we wrap ourselves in
Gloucester, an example that troubled past, doesn't have to be
    troubled future

That wounds can heal here
I stand on the land my ancestors were shackled
Breaking chains here
Gloucester
My home,
I remain here
Proud and settled in

The Human-Dinosaur Set

BY MARK GRINYER

A child in his yard plays
everywhere in anytime
with plastic toys—marvelous beasts—
dinosaurs bright in original light
triceratops and brontosauruses
galumphing and galloping under ancient stars
as children grow strong and giant at play
foreshadowing the violence that age
anger and political will make real
with bombs and bullets and charging steel.
He cannot help it—that dinosaurian roar.
It's a frightful sound young children play,
loud and ravishing as a marvelous day.
But comforting, his fellow lizards claim
without the teeth those Rexs spread
when they come charging in
to cannons firing, bombs exploding
and other sorts of human mayhem.
There's a lesson there, I believe.
Sometimes, when big beasts roar
and prance about,
where children play in streets
the little folk think some mayhem up
and put the giants to sleep.
It's a noisy world, I think,
when people and lizards meet,
and humans tend to manufacture
piles of dinosaur meat.

Coyote Caught in My Light at Night

BY MARK GRINYER

Quietly. Quietly. A moonless night. I must slip silently through these leaves. Their scent is bright. I hear rats chittering, somewhere nearby. Stop. Go silent. Be stealthy as sight. Crouch down and wait. I hear them moving, under that bush, skittering about. I smell their piss, their stinking shit. Stay slow; stay sharp; Be darkness only. Stay out of the light. The nest is nearby. A scent like heat. My teats, they ache. Sleep silently, children. Quiet as death. I'll return tonight. My need is life, these rats to eat. They are food for us. The pounce must land—like darkness with weight and teeth. So stay in place. Be still. Be silent. Wait. You are safe. My teats are aching. I leap. I've got them now. I bite. Their blood is salt-sweet. Soon you may suckle. My milk is strength. You'll drink your fill, then cuddle up tight. Quietly. Quietly. I must escape this too-bright light.

In starless darkness
the yip, yip, yips of distant
packs haunt sleepless nights.

Driving to Town with Grandpa
BY MILAN HAMILTON

I have no learning to drive memories. None of the formal driving lesson kind at least. But I remember driving to town with my grandpa. I spent summers on the farm. Part time with my Uncle Ralph, and the rest with my Grandpa Williams. Uncle Ralph (that was his name as far as I knew) taught me to drive his Farmall tractor, well enough that, at age 9, I could pull the mower or rake he sat on at haying time. Uncle Ralph paid me a dollar a day for my work, plus room and board and all the pop I could drink. Grandpa Williams never paid me, except for room and board, which was fine with me. I loved my Grandpa Williams.

My Grandpa Williams loved to go to town. And always took me with him. After the feed mill or the meat locker, we'd always stop at the town tavern, where I would be treated to my favorite, a Royal Crown Cola, aka RC. Grandpa Williams would enjoy a beer and conversation with the bartender and the other farmer who also "loved to go to town." I never kept track of how long we stayed or how many beers my grandpa consumed.

But as I have reflected on that time in my life and the many trips to town I took with Grandpa Williams, I have concluded that that is how I learned to drive. Grandpa always drove when we took his '41 Chevy two-door to town. But he always asked me if I wanted to drive that Chevy home. He would stop at the edge of town, change places with me, give me some basic instructions on how the clutch and brake worked, explain how the shift lever on the steering wheel column worked, cautioning me not to let the speedometer go over 30, and then turn me loose to drive the ten or fifteen miles back to the farm. The roads were gravel or dirt, and there was hardly ever another car, sometimes a tractor, so all I had to do was steer that Chevy down the middle of the road and avoid the ditches.

So that is how I first learned to drive a car, the result of my Grandpa Williams' love for going to town, and his knowing that he had had one too many to drive himself home. I was his backup.

He would always say: "Don't tell Grandma." That is another story.

The Candle is Us

BY MILAN HAMILTON

When my candle goes out at last
My hope is that there be more
Who have lit theirs
      From its flame
Than those who have let
      Their hopes die
While trying to live by its glow.
Darkness all around us only seems
To be the way life is
When we try to see our way
With the light of one small candle.
When we forget the real truth about life:
We are the candle who forgot
To be a conduit of the world's light,
Neither the recipient nor its source.

Bedroom
by Beverly V. Head

They moved Granny into my bedroom.
Nobody asked if I wanted to share my bedroom.
Granny slept on the twin bed next to the wall.
I slept on the twin bed next to the window in my bedroom.
She brought arthritis and Ben Gay with her.
Nobody asked if I wanted them in my bedroom.
They just moved Granny in with her aches and smells.
Nobody asked my permission to dump her in my bedroom.
This room was my book reading, looking out the window sanctuary.
I did not want to share my bedroom.
At night Granny called constantly for my mother.
I ignored her, pretending to be asleep in my bedroom.
I watched my mother take Granny to the bathroom.
Before they came back, I turned to the windows in my bedroom.
I was happy sad when my aunt took Granny to Philadelphia.
I was happier to have the solitude of my bedroom.
Now that you are old, aching, and alone, Granddaughter,
You are ashamed that you did not want to share your bedroom.

House on the Corner Lot
by Beverly V. Head

I have stood on this corner lot
With the misshapen magnolia trees
For over 60 years.
In 1961, I was new and without a family,
In this neighborhood where the streets are named after white
    English writers.
Fielding Lane, Shelly Drive, Keats Drive, Thackeray Place.
I was standing here in 1962 when the white homeowners,
Afraid of racial integration,
Persuaded the Mayor and the city Aldermen
To keep black families from moving into the neighborhood
By putting up barricades blocking entrance into the streets.
I watched black men build barriers of wood and steel
To keep out people who were black like them.
I was standing here when all barricades came down, after 72 days,
Declared unconstitutional by a judge.
I was here when black families began to move in.
I stood on this corner lot and witnessed the flight of white
    families,
Hoping to find houses away from black families.
I don't know if white families will ever come back
To Fielding Lane, Shelly Drive, Keats Drive, and Thackeray Place.
I do know I am still standing here on the corner lot
With my black family.
I am off market!

Those Damn Computers
BY RICHARD HESS

When we got our computer, the guy at the store
Said, "This thing is amazing, you'll love it, I'm sure!"

He showed with the mouse how the cursor would fly
Over the screen like a jet in the sky.

And so, the computer we wanted to buy
Couldn't wait to get home and give her a try.

Well, I turned it on – there were icons galore.
But what do they do? I wasn't so sure!

If you click on something you really don't know
It may take you somewhere you don't want to go.

If I keep going on and I'm on the wrong track
My great fear is – I won't find my way back.

So, I stare at the screen, frozen in fear
Wondering how in the world did I get here!

It is very sad, but now I can see
That I was born in the wrong century!

An Aging Body Speaks
(haiku-style)

BY CONNIE JAMESON

"Fit as a fiddle"
Were it not for my middle
Tell-tale evidence

Face the "naked truth"
Skipped exercise, extra snacks
Cannot be hidden

Poor aging body
Father Time, Mother Nature
Join forces - unfair!

Dreams of six-pack abs
Sculpted muscles, mighty strength
Better get started

Creaky knees and hips
Still get me from here to there
Just a bit later

First - marathon dreams
Next - half-marathon's just fine
Now - Yay, a full mile

How we mistreat feet
Tight shoes, stubbed toes, hot pavement
Now give pampering

Stiletto heels - Wow!
Lovely, long legs, curvy calves
But, oh, those poor feet

Lotions, potions - no!
To erase signs of aging
Just avoid mirrors

Make-up and hair dye
"You can't fool Mother Nature"
(Just want to fool Jim)

Wider stance, slow steps
Grandparent and toddler walk
What a perfect match

You call them "laugh lines"
But they make me want to cry
What a misnomer

This skin I'm in changed
Fairness, smoothness are no more
Now - saggy, baggy

Wrinkles - a road map
That can tell your Life's story
Wow! I'm well-traveled

Troubled Times
BY CECE JOHNS

Buttendiesen and Binswangen, two little Jewish communities in southern Bavaria, were very much like our little farm town, houses clustered around the synagogue and graveyard. The difference was that the Jewish families were not farmers but doing business with the farmers. Jude Rechenmacher drove around in a big Mercedes, the first in town, and bought cattle for the big city slaughterhouses. Jude Wiedeman came around with a horse and buggy to buy eggs from the farmers' wives. Traditionally, money made from things like eggs, chickens, geese and garden produce belonged to the lady of the house. Jude Schnell traded only in horses; he would not step inside a cowbarn. Jude Goldberg did his best to convince the farmers that the price he got for their sugar beet crop was the best in all of Bavaria. "Sure, sure," they all said, "he took us again this year." But nobody would think of selling his crop to someone else. Jude Eicholz was the shoemaker, Jude Weisshaupt was the tailor, and Jude Birnbaum came around on a three-wheel bicycle piled high with the beat-up suitcases. He seemed to know which day the ladies had egg money. That's when he appeared to sell them everything from buttons to sewing machine needles, from dress fabric to frying pans to romantic novels. My mother always offered Jude Birnbaum something to eat, and he always accepted. After all, my mother used to cook kosher for Jude Einstein, so therefore, it was kosher to eat in our house. His favorite was a cup of coffee and a "Bachala", not very fancy but he loved it. Coffee was "Malzkaffee" made from roasted barley. Bean coffee was only for special occasions and only in the afternoon with cake, etc. The Malzkaffee was served in a large mug with half hot milk and enough room so you could break the bread into bite size pieces into the coffee and eat it with a spoon, kind of like breakfast cereal I suppose. The Bachala was unique to my mother's hometown in "old Bavaria" and looked like an oversized French roll, about six inches in diameter, made from yeast dough, but very soft. Mama baked about two dozen every Saturday and everyone in the family had one for breakfast every day. I still remember the day in 1943 when Jude Birnbaum left one of his suitcases with my mother. After Birnbaum had gone, I asked what she had bought. She said the suitcase was for safekeeping and I was not to mention it to anyone. The suitcase disappeared and I was convinced that my mother had lied to me and that it contained our Christmas presents. It wasn't until three years later, after my mother had been killed in a bomb attack and my sister and brother had returned from the war, that I saw the suitcase again. We were getting ready to move, when during the course of packing my sister came across this locked suitcase, which neither my father nor my brother recognized, and there seemed to be no key. I arrived home from school just as my father tried to force open the lock. "This belongs to Jude Birnbaum." I said with amazement, being ashamed for thinking my mother lied to me. "He left it with mama." I said. They all looked at each other, nobody had seen Birnbaum in over three years. We all stood around his suitcase like it was a coffin containing a dear friend. Of course, by now we all knew what had happened to most of the Jews in our community, especially since Dachau was located only 20 kilometers to the south. Jude Birnbaum's valuables, entrusted to my mother's care, would never again find their rightful owner. I first became aware of goings on with our Jewish neighbors when the Sunday afternoon card games came to a halt. Unlike the Saturday night card game, which was always held in the same place, the Sunday game moved around the players' houses, mostly Jews. Sometimes my father would say, "Come on little shiksa, you can come with me." I loved it. Every house had something special, children or animals I could play with and lots of interesting food, different from our house. At tailor Weisshaupt's house I could play with boxes of buttons and fabric scraps. He once showed me how to properly install the sleeves in a doll dress I was making. And now, all of a sudden no more card games – my family whispered a lot and looked around to make sure no one was listening before discussing Jewish people. My father also started to butcher a calf along with the usual pig. Supposedly the sausages tasted better with a little added veal. The truth was he made up packages of veal and put them on the back of my bike with instructions to deliver them to certain Jewish families. My father hoped that a 9-year-old child on a bike would not be suspect. I was instructed to never stop and talk to anyone and never to go to the front door, but always to go around back. One time he packed a rucksack full of things and I was to take the little commuter train, which ran the eight km from our railroad station to Buttendwiesen. As the train served mostly the Jewish community, we called it the "Jew-Jew." It had only two passenger cars, a mail and baggage car, and the steam locomotive. I don't remember the reason for my father sending me on the train rather than the bike on that particular day, I only remember him saying, "Don't waste time, don't stop to talk or play. Go directly to Jude Weisshaupt, go to the back of the house and knock on the cellar door. You have to hurry to catch the train back." I did as I was told. I knocked on the door and there was no answer. I knocked and knocked, but the house was silent. Thinking they would return soon; I left the knapsack by the cellar door and ran back to the station only to see the back of the train in the distance. Jude Habersack's house was closest to the station, and I had seen Mrs. Habersack feeding the chickens as I ran by. I went to their back door and told them that I had missed the last train. Mrs. Habersack said she had seen me at the Weisshaupt's and if my sack contained something perishable, I had better not leave it because they were not coming home for a while. Mr. Habersack went and got the bag and offered to take me home on his bike. He avoided the main road and instead took the path through the woods. It was dark and scary. My heart was pounding in my throat as never before and our house sure looked comforting to me.

Life became more and more confusing. Every day we had news of someone dying in the war or a Jewish family disappearing. My mother kept adding new names to my bedtime prayers every night and pretty soon I was praying for everyone in our town and the next town, just to be sure I covered all the names mama had given me. Life would never be the same again.

Red Power Suit

by Margo Klein

During my working career as a CPA I often joined clients and their attorneys when they were negotiating to buy or sell a business.

One spring day I was in a conference room with my client (the seller), the buyer, three different attorneys, a business broker and two bankers. The negotiations had been going on for over an hour without much progress. Mostly I had kept silent letting the others in the room argue back and forth. But soon I knew I would have to give my opinion and try to overcome the roadblocks.

I was wearing my bright red power suit with a white sleeveless blouse underneath. Suddenly I was hit by an intense hot flash. "Menopause, not now" I thought, but positive thoughts had no effect on the raging hormones. Of course, now I was asked to speak. I got up slowly and looked at each person directly to give myself some time to pull myself together. Then I removed my suit jacket, folded it neatly and placed it on my chair.

The buyer and his attorneys looked at each other. And with a nod, they finally brought their offer to a realistic number and started negotiating in good faith. The session was a success for my client.

Later we heard from the business broker that when I stood up and took off my jacket it sent a powerful message to everyone that we wouldn't back off the selling price. I received many compliments for my negotiating technique and my power move. I never told anyone it was really just a hot flash.

Ode to my suitcase
BY MARGO KLEIN

I remember well the day we met.
Your shiny teal blue nylon pristine,
Your luggage tag gleaming
Ready for me to fill in the blanks.

Our first trip together was for business.
My professional suits and charging cables
Weighing you down
As I slipped you into the overhead bin.

More journeys followed
As we saw Greece and Ireland
Croatia and New Zealand
Taipei and Toronto, always together.

Sometimes we went to weddings
Where happy brides and grooms
Were carried around the room
To the haunting tune of the Hora.

Or to parties and showers
Where everyone's glass
overflowed with happiness
and champagne.

Three trips we made across the country
For the births of our grandchildren.
Always there for that first day
In their first home.

Once you came with me as I rushed
Straight from the plane, to the taxi,
To the hospital room.
All ended well that time.

But other, sadder times
I packed black dresses and eulogies
As I said goodbye
With red eyes and wringing hands.

Now both of us are showing
Wear and tear and strain.
But don't worry, if our paths must deviate,
I'll meet up with you by the pearly gate.

In the ICU, 10/12/2018

by Robin Longfield

I

Detective Raymond, outside your ICU box—
blue-black uniform, waits like death, waits for
death, listens for monitors to silence,
for the sounds of broken hearts— sobs and wails
from the other side of the curtain. Night
falls without notice. He chats with a nurse,
looks at his phone, the clock, his phone again.
Someone offers him a See's Chocolate-
Inside and outside your room, the waiting
continues, the waiting for your ending.

II

I imagined death as an entity,
waiting like in old movies—impatient
as the driver of *The Phantom Carriage*,
or, Mr. Brink, fooled into that ancient
apple tree, by cunning, old, Lionel
Barrymore, in *On Borrowed Time*, but you,
you, had no love for black and white movies—
preferring death and vengeance delivered
by Keanu Reeves as John Wick— direct
bloody, in vivid colors. This was one
of the many differences between us.
What else did you know? What do you know now?

III

For once, I don't know anything, only how
to feel—a nerve uncovered, caught in wind,
trying to hold together, automotron
in a centrifuge of grief, falling
apart, spun together again, again
in a gravitron of time. Neighbors with
the code word come in and out of your space—
relatives call from afar—their voices
translate into the language of birds. I
can't understand a thing except this:
the code word is all we can control.

IV

I hold your hand and peer through the curtain—
Detective Raymond waits, looks at his phone
again, watches the clock, waits to claim
his evidence. I sense the presence
of an owl behind me but cannot turn
around. Detective Raymond waits, waits—
The code word is all we can control.

A revised version of this poem appears in the Inlandia Journal Fall 2025.

Words of Wisdom
BY ROBIN LONGFIELD

Many years ago, during a coming-of-age ceremony at church, I was asked to impart wisdom to a group of teenage girls, including my eldest daughter. The words I chose had nothing to do with the type of worship or faith professed within a sanctuary. But, they were words of faith. "Know your worth" and "Believe in yourself" were what I said to every young girl who came to my place in the circle of wise women who were charged with saying profound things to these high school-aged girls. If I had then known the saying, " Women who settle for less than they deserve end up with less than they settled for," I would have told them that as well.

In my own young life, and in the lives of so many other women, having someone tell us words like that may have saved us from decisions made in haste, out of fear, or from the belief no other alternatives existed. Some consequences we experienced were merely inconveniences; others led to stifled lives in which our true, beautiful selves were imprisoned in glass cocoons. Some of us emerged to stretch our wings and, indeed, fly. Others emerged with wings that never entirely dried straight. Still others never appeared. Some of us made choices of a more deadly nature, living life as if it required traversing a burning tightrope without a safety net.

Growing up in the 1960s and 70s, positive, empowering role models and mentors for little girls were nearly non-existent within my family. It was very much a "boys will be boys" attitude toward my brother, and my gifts were often downplayed to prevent me from becoming "big-headed" or outshining him. I suspect I was not an isolated case. I was fortunate to have a handful of highly encouraging teachers, and I will never stop being grateful for them. But, what is the lesson we learn as children when our families cannot bring themselves to acknowledge the beauty and worthiness of their daughters? The kind of beauty and worthiness that are not contingent on talent, athletic ability, good grades, or, simply being "good"

That was why I said those carefully chosen words to all the young girls who were "bridging" that day. That is why I told them to my daughters. That is why I tell them to myself now. Had I heard them from my own family, I may have made decisions with a more rational mind, with the faith that better things (jobs, for instance) were on the horizon. That I was worth the wait. For everything this crazy, wild, beautiful, banquet of a world lays before us if we are only brave enough to approach the groaning table and fix ourselves a plate. A big plate.

Hiding Out at the B & G

by James Luna

Frank and Jesse James. Al Capone and Frank Nitti. Ronnie and me. All great evaders of the law. No disrespect intended, but the others bloomed late. Ronnie and I got our start in elementary school.

Fourth grade. 1970 something. If you missed the 70's, you didn't miss much. In San Bernardino, smog alerts most of the year made playing any sport and being outside a form of self-harm. Indoors, cumulus clouds of cigarette smoke hung in restaurants, stores, schools and hospitals. I always found it funny when people would share the ages they started smoking, since we were exposed to second-hand smoke at birth. Lastly, in the 70's, if you were lucky, you could get about seven TV channels that were on between 5:00 a.m. and midnight; IF you lived near a major metropolis and the Santa Ana winds weren't bending the aerial antenna.

If you miss the 70's, I get it. The stars in the desert were never clearer than when I lay in the back of a pickup rolling down Interstate 10. After school was for riding bikes or football in the street without interruption. As far as distractions, the only family notifications were when my mom yelled out the window to come home for dinner.

I was 9, and Ronnie was 8 (He'd been moved up a grade because he was so smart.). We were in what is now called GATE (Gifted and Talented Education). The gift we got was that every Wednesday, he and I and Irma Diaz were put on a bus and sent across town for enrichment time. Usually, we sat in silence, watching the landscape change from views of cars on cinder blocks and ceramic toucans to the world of topiary bushes and golf courses. The 70's were also the years when schools tried to make up for being lame by sending some of their students to richer, less-lame schools. Look up the videos. You'll see kids of color as they are infected with the virus of trauma. Fortunately for us, our rides were quiet and uneventful.

We were dropped off at Parkside Elementary (I never saw the park on the side. Districts give schools weird names. Mt. View Elementary has a view of Mount Rubidoux; not quite a mountain.) There, a room was set aside for "enrichment", which is teacher talk for "interesting". Science kits, shelves of books, art sets, and other rarities not found on San Bernardino's West Side filled the room. However, the education methodology of that class still baffles me. As a teacher for 39 years, I never encountered the system used in our crosstown class. In a word: nothing! We were never taught anything. There was a teacher in the room, but he didn't teach lessons. Instead, we were left on our own, with the expectation that we would choose what we wanted to learn. The catch was we had to teach ourselves. As a teacher for 39 years, I never encountered a system based on nothing. I still have the journal from those years. There are no enlightening entries, and the only interesting memory I recall is getting 77 out of 100 on the ESP cards. I do remember we never had recess. Another gift to the gifted.

Most of the time, we felt like ghosts in another person's house, wishing we were back at Riley Elementary, in our familiar class with our friends.

One Wednesday, I met Ronnie when the bus dropped him off.

Without even a "hey" he jumped right into his scheme. "Let's ditch the class today."

"Ditch? No way!" I said in my best Catholic boy voice.

Ronnie shook his head. "Not the whole day, just Parkside."

"How?"

Like most ideas, there was no plan behind it. We stood outside the school gates for a moment, then Ronnie yelled, "I got it!" He pointed across the street. "Let's go across the street to the B & G. We'll wait there till the bus that takes us to Parkside leaves. Then we go to school. We'll just tell them that we got there late."

It was genius. I could see how Ronnie got moved up a grade. Though leaving school after arriving felt like a prison break. I looked around for teachers or supervisors. No one was around. Now was our only chance.

I pulled a wrinkled bill from my pocket. "I got a dollar," I said. "I'll get us some candy."

The plan put a proverbial pep in our step, though we made sure to cross the street quickly, out of sight of the office windows.

The B & G was across the street from Riley Elementary (B & G stood for Baseline and G Street. That name made sense. To this day, I don't know who the namesake of our school, Riley is.). After a few minutes, the bell rang three times, sending our classmates in. However, the bus to Parkside wouldn't get to our school for another 5 minutes. We initiated Step 2, entering the B & G to kill time. The owner usually shooed kids out except when they had money. I held my dollar in my hand to show him we meant business. So, he didn't bother us, or care that we were

supposed to be in class. We strolled the aisles slowly, like millionaires at yacht sales. When Ronnie nodded, I bought a Snickers for me and Oh, Henry! for him. We left the store.

"Wait here. I'll check," Ronnie said. He peered around the corner. "The bus is there." He paused. "There goes Mirna." I heard the bus pull away. "All clear," Ronnie announced. We congratulated ourselves at having evaded a dull morning. Though there was a bit of a sting when I thought of poor Mirna riding a huge yellow bus by herself to Parkside. However, a Snickers bar at 8:45 a.m. heals many pains.

Ronnie and I crossed Baseline, got to school and went to the office. The secretary glared at us.

"You're late," she scolded.

"Who's late?" the principal asked, leaving his office. My heart raced. Mr. Peterson had struck fear in me since the day in second grade when he grabbed my arm and told me to finish my lunch. Finishing lunch was a misdemeanor compared to ditching class. Ronnie and I were Class A felons now. Mr. Peterson froze when he saw us.

"The bus just left," he announced, as if we didn't know.

"Yeah, well, we woke up late," Ronnie explained.

Mr. Peterson looked at the clock. He went to his office and grabbed his coat. "Come on." Then he told the secretary, "I'll be right back."

I thought he was taking us to class, instead, he held the door open and motioned for us to go outside. Stunned but obedient, we left the office. He walked us to his car. "Get in," he ordered.

Ronnie and I looked at each other. Where were we going? To the police department? To juvey? Mr. Peterson grumbled as he drove. "I hope you appreciate my effort. You're fortunate to experience what Parkside has to offer. Your classmates would love to do what you're doing."

Stifling the obvious question, "Then why don't we have those things at Riley?" I looked ahead. Ronnie too kept quiet. Mr. Peterson continued mumbling, but my dread of my parents' punishment and any school discipline left me deaf. As he led us to the Parkside office, he scolded, "Now you listen to me. If you ever try anything like this again, I'll call your parents!"

Next time? I thought. No consequence? No one will know? I finally exhaled and nodded.

As Ronnie and I walked quickly to class, he whispered. "Next week, we'll hide in the bathroom till the bus leaves."

Back In The Old Days
BY MERRIL LYEW

Elsie sat on the porch in her old rocking chair and sighed. The air carried a faint scent of mothballs. "Back in my days," she said in her trembling voice, "children knew their place. Respect for elders, that's what's missing these days."

Her granddaughter, Lily, rolled her eyes. "Grandma, it was different back then. People walked everywhere, there were no phones, no internet..."

Elsie scoffed. "That's nonsense!" she declared. "We had community. Neighbors looked out for each other. Kids played outside until the streetlights came on, not glued to some glowing screen."

There was a lot of noise coming from the backyard. A young boy from the neighborhood, tears streaming down his face, stumbled into the yard. He had fallen off his bike, and his knees were bleeding.

Lily rushed to help. Neighbors came out of their houses, offering bandages and support. Elsie, observing the scene, smiled for the first time in a long time. "Things aren't so different after all," she thought.

I always thought I'd see you again
BY ANNE MALCOLM

I always thought I would see you again. Despite the evidence of my senses. Despite seeing the blood stained shower stall where you'd sheltered, and must have known you were trapped. Before fire robbed the air of oxygen, filling it with smoke, and you fell to the floor.

Blood seeping from wounds to an already lifeless body.

I always thought I would see you again. Despite walking the smoke filled corridors. Fire still smoldering in adjacent rooms. Despite seeing your belongings on the bedside table. Picking up your contact lens case and the last book you read. Clutching them tightly, knowing you would want them soon. Next week, you'll need them, when the site survey ends, and you return to our home.

Remarkable really that I was allowed in the building. Dangerous and unstable as it was.

Testament to the kindness of the dark haired man with hooked nose and gentle brown eyes. Or perhaps to the wildly unhinged appearance of my sleep deprived self, as I emerged from the State Department car. Or testament possibly to the privilege of being a white woman, in a developing country, in an unequal world.

To this day the smell of beef jerky assaults my nostrils and flashes me back to dark corridors. The beam of a flashlight, air heavy with the scent of smoke and burnt flesh. But you didn't burn. Your body was still whole. I saw you in the press photo carried aloft by four grim faced Arab men. Pushing through gallibaya clad crowds, there to witness mass death, or perhaps searching for loved ones themselves. Your big toe peeping from the sheet shroud in which you were wrapped. I knew that toe well. From endless days frolicking in our joyful marriage bed.

Endless weekends watching you running bare foot in warm sand and planting those toes and feet firmly on the sailboard as you caught the gust and sped into the blue, ahead of the wind.

Endless days. Endless weeks, months and years we would have together. We naively imagined, with the envisioned indestructibility of youth.

Always, despite all the evidence stacking up against it. I thought that I would see you again.

Later I returned to the other hotel, and found your sister hunched fetal in a closet. Crying quietly like an animal hiding spooked in a cave. And I crawled in beside her and we rocked together, screaming soundlessly, drowning in tears, gulping air, maddened by grief.

And we knew we wouldn't make it through, unless we could see you again.

Waking from sedated sleep, panicked, bolting upright, I grabbed the bedside phone. You'd dream called me and I knew I must get to the morgue. But they wouldn't let me go to you.

Wait they said, wait. Wait till tomorrow. Then, wait till repatriation. Then, wait till the funeral. But they never let me see you again. Complicating my grief.

Months later, I saw you one day, back stateside. Walking with the crowd along a bustling beach town sidewalk. Powerful shoulders, a head taller than the throng, blonde surfer hair reflecting light. Crossing the road I was aware of brakes squealing, cars honking as I followed you at a run. Then he turned, and his profile spoke of the lie, I was telling myself, still.

"I know I will see you again".

Years later you came to a dear friend in a dream. You'd told her to tell me good news.

That life is a banquet, a grand sequential array, of delicious courses served in an endless Summer of plenty and delight. Ours was just the first course, you had said. Carry on, experience every dish life has to offer. And I smiled at her effort, and tried.

I Tried and I tried, to do as I was told.

But the other courses, they all tasted of cardboard and sand, and none has been as delicious as the first dish we shared. Thirty years ago. Half a lifetime past.

And still I wait to see you again.

Still I wait to be with you again.

How I long to be with you again.

My one true love.

My Childhood Home
by Mae Wagner Marinello and Betty Wagner Randolph

(Note: on the week this prompt was given, my sister, Betty, was in town and wrote her version of "My Childhood Home." Her words are interspersed among mine in italics.)

We had a pretty big house—compared to some. We lived in a little town in Southwest North Dakota.

I don't think I realized how unique my home was when I was a child. It had been a church in another life; back then, I don't think I realized all homes didn't come with a "churchpart"—all one word. My parents must have christened it when we moved in because I never remember a time when it was not the churchpart. I took it for granted, just like a kitchen is taken for granted.

There were my parents, Alice Mae and Budd, two brothers, Stan and Paul, my sister, Mae, and me. We had three bedrooms, one closet and one bathroom; it consisted of a bathtub, toilet and a small dresser. It had no sink. For several years we had no hot water in the house. My sister and I would share the bathtub—but first we had to heat water on the stove and carry the big speckled blue kettle of water into the bathroom and pour it in the bathtub. One time when we carried it to the bathroom, it got spilled and my sister burned her leg with the hot water.

The churchpart was adjacent to the basement—the basement housed the coal furnace and my mother's wringer washing machine, along with two metal rinse tubs on legs. There was a step-up door that led to the garage and a step-down door that led to the fragrantly earthy root cellar. There was another door to the churchpart; it was a large room that ran the length of the house with a raised section for the organ and pulpit.

The middle part of the house was the parsonage. The upper-most level was an unfinished attic; it had a window at the north end and a window at the south end. It, like the parsonage and churchpart, ran the length of the house.

We had white maple floors that my dad was extremely proud of—but they were nearly covered with big sheets of linoleum.

When we moved in, there was also a wooden outhouse set far back from the house. Although the outhouse was one building, it had a wooden partition in the middle; one side for ladies, and the other side for men. Luckily, we never had to use the outhouse because the parson and his family had a bathroom in the house with a toilet and tub!

I wish I knew more about the story of the house and its history as a church. For more than seven years, I wrote a column for the *Adams County Record*, Hettinger's local weekly newspaper. A man told me he was researching the days when it was a church; unfortunately, he passed away and I don't know what happened to his research.

I also wish I knew how it was that my parents were able to buy it because we seemed to have so little money; I think there were times when they were on the brink of losing it. Prior to moving to the former church, we lived in a tiny house down the hill.

Our house was a magical playground for my sister, Betty, and me. We had so many different places we could play. First, we could play in the churchpart—I remember playing store there with wooden crates for store shelves and a black grease pen that must have come from the Super Valu grocery store as my mother used one to mark prices on canned foods and such when she worked there. For years, some of the toys we played with bore the prices Betty and I placed on them.

In the attic, we played dress-up with old clothes and dolls. The attic also seemed to be our favorite place to play "paper dolls out of the catalog" –perhaps because we didn't have to pick them up each time like we would have had to do if we played with them on the main floor. With the Sears Christmas catalog, Betty and I could give our paper doll families all the toys and clothes we might have wished we could have—but couldn't. I don't think we realized just how poor we were in those days—but we were rich in our imaginations. We were so lucky! And, at Christmas my mother always seemed to see to it that we would each get one special gift that we chose from the catalog.

The biggest problem with the attic was that it was too hot in the summer and too cold in the winter to play there – but it proved its usefulness in another way. When our mother couldn't hang the laundry outside in the winter, she carried heavy baskets up the dangerous basement stairs where there was no handrail. (One time, I fell over the side of those stairs onto the cement floor of the basement.) There was another set of stairs up into the main floor, then more stairs up to the attic. Clotheslines were strung from one end of the attic to the other – where sometimes, the laundry still froze stiff. That's how cold it was!

We didn't have much money. My mother worked at the hospital, different restaurants and the Super Valu grocery store. My dad trapped furs and did some farming. We were quite poor—I remember having butter and sugar or ketchup sandwiches for lunch. My mom would put together a good supper for us – then, we younger siblings would wash and dry the supper dishes. Our brother, Stan was always working. The rest of us also worked from a young age.

Betty and I also liked to play with the sexy Mopsy paper dolls that we cut from the Sunday edition of the Minneapolis St. Paul Tribune. I loved drawing clothes for Mopsy and store-bought paper dolls. I drew for children I babysat as well.

We had some cold weather in Dakota. The last winter I lived there, it got down to minus 46 degrees—and that was before the factored in wind chill! The following summer my mom, Mae and I moved from North Dakota to Riverside, California. Our parents divorced.

Although it was never the same, I was happy to return to my Hettinger home and spend two or three summers with my dad and two brothers.

As for me, I graduated from Poly High School in Riverside in 1959 and got married the same year. When my husband was discharged from the Marines, we traveled to his home state of Illinois via North Dakota. I made a few more visits while my dad was still alive. He lived alone in that big old house until he passed away. After his death, my brother, Paul remodeled the house, turning it into three apartments; it was later sold to Anne, a widow with four daughters. She had fallen in love with the house when she worked there during a time when it was used as a day care facility. It is no longer divided into apartments but went back to being a single-family home when Anne bought it. She and I bonded over the house and remain friends to this day. When I returned to Hettinger for an All-School Reunion and Centennial, she welcomed me to stay with her. Another time, both Betty and I stayed there in one of the bedrooms in what had been the churchpart. What a gift that was for us!

Perhaps there were echoes of the years we spent in our special childhood home; Anne told me it was as if she had sensed our presence in the house before she ever met me. She was also happy to eventually meet Betty and Paul; Stan had passed away years before.

Anne's husband had died in a tragic farm accident; I am so happy that the house welcomed her and her daughters and that someone who loves the house still lives there. Even though she never met him, she planted a tree in memory of my dad and has sent pictures of its growth progress now and then. I also gave her a picture of him. It means so much to me that she honors him in this way.

Yes, my childhood home was unique. I am very happy for the years that I was privileged to live there.

The Fountain of Youth?
by Elisse Martinez

On a sunny spring afternoon I attended a charity luncheon. The fragrance from the floral centerpieces, striking with pastel pinks and lavenders, welcomed me. Before long I observed an old acquaintance. "Could that be Cloe?" I wondered. Her fine reputation as a landscape artist was well deserved. She looked wonderful and refreshed for her 85 years.

I crossed the room and greeted Cloe, admiring her healthy look. She turned to introduce me to Joy, who had been a Hollywood makeup artist. She had given Cloe a makeover, and I inquired if she would be available for me. The beautiful Joy, with a glowing complexion and long wavy gray hair, handed me her card. "Call me soon," she warned, "as I will have knee surgery in a few weeks."

Makeup was not a priority for me during my years of teaching elementary school. I did not wish to fuss each morning on being glamorous, but I did use lipstick, eyebrow pencil and blush. I also began coloring graying hairs in my 40s.

Society's pressures to look younger are prevalent in America and now affect more young, middle aged and old aged women, as well as men. We are bombarded by ads on TV, social media and magazines to appear more youthful. The majority of my 50-year-old daughter's friends have had a cosmetic procedure, including Botox, facelifts, microneedling, tattooed eyebrows and much more.

My daughter has remained aloof to these pressures. She wishes to grow old gracefully and show the natural age lines from years of working and raising four children. They are well deserved marks of honor.

Americans worship at the altar of youth now more than ever. The cosmetic industry makes $648 billion a year in the US alone just on products, not procedures. A twenty-four-year-old family friend, who loves her job as a registered nurse, told me recently that she is going for a Master's Degree in cosmetology due to the large increase in salary she will make working with a plastic surgeon.

Aah, but I digress. Joy scheduled an appointment with me at Macy's in Victoria Gardens, as they have an exceptional cosmetic department. When we entered the first floor my eyes widened in amazement. I was speechless. The entire floor sold only cosmetics. There were dozens and dozens of displays.

Joy perused the counters and chatted with a few stunning makeup artists. A beautiful Caribbean woman named Mae, with café-au-lait skin and a dark bun, was selected. I was seated in a high, comfortable chair while Mae looked me over. She gathered several creams and ointments in gorgeous packaging with alluring names. Marketing is very clever, and embellishes the products to appeal to our sense of youth.

The procedure began by cleansing my face and pulling my hair back with a headband. Joy took a "before" photo with my cell phone. Mae explained each product as she gently applied the serums to my face. At one point I observed Joy smiling and nodding yes, noticing results between certain applications. There were nine products with names like "Bye-Bye Lines," "Confidence in a Cream," "PhotoFinish," names to capture one's hopes and dreams of youth. Products are international in scope, from France, U.S., England and Canada.

The process was complete in about 40 minutes. An "after" photo was taken. Comparing the two photos, there was a dramatic change. The makeup artist had transformed my face into a fresher, younger looking woman.

Mae was patient and helped me complete a list of the steps so I might be successful at home. I have succumbed to the vanity of our era, and added to the profits of the international cosmetics industry. I am sad and happy all at once.

Grandpa Ray

BY ELISSE MARTINEZ

Stories about my quiet, anti-social Grandpa Ray were passed down from one generation to the next. Ray was a robust Russian Jew with a weathered complexion and a handsome square face His body was strong and muscular from twelve hours of farm work daily as a boy. He would ask you to try and punch his stomach and then laugh heartily when you found resistance hard as a rock. He was often unshaven with a short haircut. His hands and nails were nearly black from hard labor. Scruffy, solemn and very intelligent would describe how I remember him.

Raymond grew up in a poor shtetl in the countryside. The esteemed Rabbi taught Hebrew and history to the bright boys. Frequent offers were made by the Rabbi and his wife, who were childless, to adopt Ray. They tried to make the case that he could have a better life and become a Rabbi. His parents refused, as he was their only son out of five children. He was a quick learner who spoke five languages: Russian, Polish, Hebrew, Yiddish and later English.

In the year 1900, at age 16, Grandpa Ray was conscripted into the harsh Russian army. To avoid service, his family advised him to leave Russia for America. Later he could send for them. Aunt Rachel was already in America and would sponsor him. The family was fortunate to all leave right before the deadly pogroms began. He escaped in the middle of the night and walked carrying loaves of dark bread, apples, a jug of water, and the small savings allotted to him. He reached the sea and boarded a ship to America. He settled in Buffalo, New York. The climate reminded him of his homeland. He peddled scraps and rags for a living. Later he worked on Singer sewing machines and began selling and servicing them. This brought him a comfortable income.

In his mid-20s he met pretty, petite Rose Kaiser at a dance. They married a little later and raised three daughters. They all learned to sew on a treadle machine and made much of their clothing. The youngest, Elaine, became a skilled dressmaker. When I was eight years old, Elaine's husband Dan was home from the war. He had been in France during the liberation, and brought home a huge red Nazi flag. Aunt Elaine used it to sew several items, among them a Red Riding Hood costume for me at Halloween. I adored the costume but never knew until much later of its notorious origin!

Healthy living habits were natural to Grandpa Ray. Bushel baskets brimming with apples, pears, onions, potatoes and any fruit in season were stored in his basement. He consumed them raw, in sauces, juices or canned by the dozens for the winter. I can still taste the sweet canned cherries and peaches.

Ray drove a Model A Ford, which he kept running for several years. On occasion he would pick me up from elementary school. I was so embarrassed by the old car that I asked him to wait on the corner. Now that I am an adult, I realize how much heart he put into the car. I would admire the car and run out of school to meet him!

The Best Place to Live
by Terry Lee Marzell

The best place to live is…

- A place where neighbors accept each other, and respect each other, and are kind to each other, and where taking care of each other has a higher priority than accumulating individual wealth;

- A place of wonder, joy, and peace;

- A place where the basic needs of every person are met: food, housing, and health care;

- A place where introspection and personal growth are valued more than ambition, and where integrity and good citizenship are valued more than glitz and glamor;

- A place where people can be trusted so completely and conditions are so safe that measures of defense are rendered unnecessary;

- A place where the governments of nations work diligently to establish and preserve human rights for all their citizens, and to improve the everyday lives of their citizens, rather than to solidify power and wealth in the hands of a privileged few;

- A place where national and international resources are used to build centers of learning, beneficial scientific inquiry, art, and culture instead of weapons;

- A place where the animals, plants, elements, and processes of nature are valued, safe-guarded, and nurtured;

- A place where we acknowledge that the mysteries of the Divine are true, and that *more* is also true.

This is the best place to live, and this is the place where I want to live.

Remembering Mom-Pain and Grief

BY ROSE Y. MONGE

Ring, ring, ring, ring, ring. I hesitate in answering the phone since I'm running late to my exercise class at Curves. I'm already half way through the door but decide to answer the phone.
It's my older sister, Mary who is out of breath and sounds distressed. It surprises me since she rarely calls me .Come and get me. Come and get me, she keeps repeating in an anxious voice. Slow down and tell me what's going on, I respond. Seconds pass as she gains her composure. We need to get to Mom's house now she blurts out but I can't talk now. I'll meet you outside my apartment and please hurry, she adds and then hangs up. What is going on, I ponder.

No time to change out of my sneakers, sweats and T-shirt and I get into my van. I make record time getting to her apartment since she lives close by. As we drive to Mom's home in Rubidoux, Mary is furious with youngest brother Bill, who lives with Mom. The story is that Bill gets home early from his postal route and finds Mom on the laundry room floor. Did he call an ambulance, I ask. No, but he keeps telling me that Mom doesn't want an ambulance, Are you kidding me, I retort. What is he thinking?

We arrive and enter Mom's house. Bill is still in a panic mode repeating that Mom told him not to call an ambulance. It breaks my heart to see Mom on the floor trying to hold back tears. I lean down to comfort her. Mary orders Bill to get her wheel chair and chastises him for not calling the ambulance or 911.

We clean Mom up the best we can as I notice vomit on her gown and floor. She keeps apologizing for putting us in this situation. She doesn't object when we tell her that we're taking her to the emergency room at Parkview Hospital, I feel helpless. I'm glad that Mary has medical experience as a nurse being an LVN before retiring. Let's call 911, I suggest. No time to waste, Mary contends. We can make faster time if we take her ourselves. I don't agree but Mary insists.

We carefully place Mom in Bill's car and I tell them that I will follow them in my van. It's the height of rush hour on the 91 freeway and there's an accident slowing people down. I lose sight of Bill's car. . I arrive at Parkview but circle around several times for a parking spot. Finally, a parking spot! I make my way to the emergency waiting room.

What a chaotic scene! It's small, noisy and crowded! Every seat is taken. It's a microcosm of humanity-both young and old. Some are wearing face masks due to the current surge of the swine flu. I have no choice but stand near the edge of the entry door and wait for Bill to arrive.

Mary completes the necessary paperwork in another area. Some children are crying; others scamper around spontaneously. I suspect than many have been there for hours. Parents try to quiet the children to no avail. Many are slumped in their chair; others have their eyes closed looking sullen.

The paperwork completed, we wait in the small intake area next to the waiting room. Mary tries to coax Mom into drinking some water. Mom's afraid that she will throw up again as she had done earlier. I moisten her lips with a water-soaked paper towel. We have no idea if she has eaten anything today. As Mom is diabetic, Mary takes her blood sugar count; gasps and spews a curse word. She stomps towards an attendant and demands immediate medical attention as she relays Mom's blood sugar level. The attendant looks startled but acts accordingly. Without hesitation, she opens the double doors and takes Mom to another room. We learn later that her blood sugar level is three times the average level.

As we wait, I think about Mom and her health-related issues. I worry about her constantly. She is diabetic, has hyper-tension, a thyroid condition and advanced arthritis. Fifteen years ago, she is diagnosed with inoperable brain aneurysms which she controls with medication.

You can understand that any change in her medical condition is a major concern for the family.

My sister and I stay with Mom as they proceed to evaluate her in a restricted area. This room has 8 beds with very little privacy. Only moveable overhead plastic curtains separate the beds. The extent of activity is mindboggling reminding me of the television show-ER. Mom gets a bed next to a young man who is the focus of activity. Staff members come and go to attend him at regular intervals. I learn later that the young man is being treated for a drug overdose.

On the other side of the room, a young woman weeps across the room, asking for pain medication but nobody attends to her. She picks up cell phone yelling at someone on the screen. She demands that someone give her Vicodin and continues crying uncontrollably. Finally, an attendant responds to her but she continues berating and complaining about the hospital staff.

They finally remove her out of the room.

Several staff members come and go attending to Mom. I lose track of the time but was glad that Mom is given pain medication. Afterwards, they take her to get X-Ray's. We continue to wait.

She is diagnosed with a fractured right hip. We learn later that due to her arthritis, her knees had buckled causing her fall. My poor mom had been on the floor since the early morning unable to move. Additionally, she injures her elbow as she attempts to break her fall.

I go outside to get some fresh air. I see my sister Norma and my niece Miranda outside waiting to get a seat in the emergency room. I undate Mom's diagnosis. By now it's getting dark and realize I haven't eaten since this morning. I decide to go to pick up some fast food. Norma calls the other siblings who plan to arrive later.

I buy plenty of food and return to the hospital. Norma updates Mom's status. She can have surgery the following day if her vitals are stabilized. We breathe a sigh of relief. As we eat, we agree to learn more about Mom's medical issues. Since I'm retired, I'm available to take Mom to her medical appointments. Mary doesn't drive and the rest of the siblings have full-time jobs

Mom has hip surgery the following day as scheduled. Her operation is successful by all accounts but her recovery is painful and takes months. She's transferred for physical therapy at Reche Canyon Rehabilitation Center in Colton. The Center is considered one of the best for her type of injury.

On Mother's Day 2009, the family gathers at the Reche Center. It's a new experience for us since we always celebrate at Mom's home. What a great celebration! We bring food to share and spend several hours reminiscing about our younger days. Mom beams with pride seeing the "Chulada de Monges" around her. The "chulada" is Dad's loving nickname for our family and the term is hard to translate. Let's say that for us, it means the "beautiful brood of Monges."

After her stay at Reche Canyon, Mom returns home but she's not the same. The months that follow are stressful with constant medical appointments and hospital stays. I reflect on Mom's accident over the years since her passing in 2011. The last family event she attends is my niece's Rosita's wedding in San Francisco in 2010. Mom looks so happy in the wedding photos.

Life is fragile. Each of us cope with grief in our own fashion after the loss of our parents. Losing Dad in 1994 is difficult but we had Mom to buffer the loss. Does it get easier over time? Perhaps. I miss my parents each and every day. Some memories last for a lifetime and surface often at the most unexpected moments. I find that writing about my parents' love and influence on my life somewhat eases the pain of losing them,

.

Hate

by Barbara Mortensen

Hate is such an interesting four-letter word. It is usually a negative word, used when you don't want to do something like. "I hate this assignment, I hate going to the doctor, I hate to tell you this bad news. It can and often does connote a negative feeling for a person or a thing. "I hate this person" I hate this idea" or" I hate doing the dishes."

I could probably write at least a page or two of all the ways the word hate is used.

However, I would hate to do that so instead. What would happen if we changed the word Hate from an action or a feeling word to an acronym? Could or would it change its negative connotation?

What would the acronym stand for?

Here are some suggestions:

> H= Honesty. Happiness
> A=affability, Ability
> T=Tenacity, thoughtfulness
> E= Empathy or Efficiency

What a difference don't you agree?

Imagine if the acronym with all the positive words you could assign to it. was used around the world? I HATE to say it but, I think we would all be in a happier more peaceful world.

Handpicked

BY SAVANNAH MUÑOZ

Hair ribbons, kittens nuzzling your hand,
and that baby blue painting he made for you,
a painting you hang in your room.
Fresh curtains, your knitting needles clicking,
and the smell of your favorite smushed lipstick
that lost its cap in your pocket.
Pale mornings, perfume spritzing your skin,
and the tall wooden case he made for your books,
the rabbit vase next to Virginia Woolf.
Your niece's peach fuzz shiny on her cheeks, you nuzzle her
on the well-worn recliner your grandmother left behind.
Your mother's stained hair dye boxes, her bangles of turquoise
and jade she wears for good luck. Sweet pea body spray you
wore in high school, the same scent on your neck when
you met your golden puppy, now gone gray.
The sorrow, the relief, when you take off your shoes and walk on
warm grass. The music box from your father that lost its music and
its dancer. The pressure of your kitten dozing on your chest. The
    sunflowers
your aunt left on your grandmother's dining table. The price of your
grandmother's shiny headstone, the one you paid for
all alone. And the fridge full of food she bought
only you get to eat.

Snare

by Savannah Muñoz

And with the spring comes a frenzy/ and a snare lassoed round my wrist/ a trap of braided hair/ impervious/ luring me to the house atop a hill/ where coyotes hunt house cats/ and stray chickens/ and my memory.

Here/ the gray-haired ancient magic in me/ hums and drones beneath my skin/ and I feel brand new/ brand new again.

Here/ my grandmother and my grandfather fell/ snares of their own/ snapped/ fraying/ sundered/ their threadbare magic still flickering at the edges/ a cigarette end flaring red.

Bodies built for somewhere else/ but not here.

Here/ I learn of my quandary/ it is not magic/ nor a curse/ but a snare that tugs me/ makes me tumble/ headfirst and/ hurried and/ it will live in my bones/ long past my departure.

We three set out in search of peace/ our bodies lacking natural calm/ our hands shaky/ our breath on tenterhooks/ we must fix it with an illicit element/ they picked poison and/ I picked feed.

Mine was the safest and still I/ slept among fruit flies and/ rotting food and/ dreams half-dreamt and/ only I still stand.

Hospitals

BY GARY NEUHARTH

Hospitals are a mixed experience for me. I remember when I was young, about ten years old, I had my tonsils taken out. They put me out with ether and when I woke up, they gave me ice cream to eat. I loved that experience – a lot.

Later, when I was older and working in the yard, I got a cut on my knee and it got infected; they couldn't find an antibiotic that would stop the infection. My wife and sister came to visit me. They sang hymns at my bedside – I didn't like that visit because I got the impression that they thought I was going to die there.

I recovered.

Later in life, I fell off my racing bike and they fixed my hip with rods in the bone to my knee and rods to anchor it at the hip. They put me in bed for several days. I wanted to go to the bathroom, about ten feet away– but a nurse from India told me I could not leave the bed for anything. I thought this was severe so I told the nurse I would not be responsible for what I would do to her if she tried to stop me. She kept her place, and I went to the bathroom

Afterwards I felt bad about having my own way.

Another time, I was in Redlands Community Hospital to have a knee looked at. I heard a woman calling out, — "God help me, someone help me!" She kept calling out but no one came to answer her. I felt sorry for her and asked the nurse if she heard her calling– she had been calling out for more than an hour. I asked why no one had come to answer her or check on her or attempt to soothe her. The nurse said she was crazy, so they just left her alone. I didn't like the answer. It made trying to help a futile experience. I felt being a nurse like that was only a self-serving experience. After all, we are human beings and should sympathize with others who need help.

When I was in Chattanooga, Tennessee at a self-supporting institution called Wildwood, I was assigned to help "Mr. Boem" in a cottage behind their sanitarium. The nurses said he was crazy, but they never explained it to me.

When I saw him, he said a dog bit his fingers off. He had to be fed, showered and was kept in bed a lot. I told Mr. Boem I loved him and helped him many times. One day, I asked him how he got there, and he told me his story. His relatives had brought him there and dumped him off and drove away. They did not contact him or visit him after that.

I talked to him after that every day, and little by little, we even prayed together at each visit. About a month later, I left for California – but Mr. Boem was a new person – really changed. He was feeding himself, bathing and walking again. He was outside and planting flowers around his cottage.

Mr. Boem was a miracle to me. God had worked a miracle and all it took was just a little love in his life.

An Eastside Introduction to the Arts

BY DEBORAH NEVÁREZ

Last year, while conducting genealogical research, my nerdy adult version of an Easter egg hunt, reviewing endless sheets of microfiche until my eyeballs ached, I came across an article in the Belvedere Citizen/Eastside Journal dated December 3, 1970, the year I turned five. As Gomer Pyle, USMC of my childhood TV land, I felt myself whisper under my breath: "Sur-prise, sur-prise, sur-prise." Might there have been another little Deborah (named of course, after Deborah Kerr, so that she may aspire to become "a lady") in the East Los Angeles of 1970? Apparently, my mother, Anglophile and lover of the arts that she still is, had enrolled her only daughter in a dramatic arts class for "Eastside children" (the article emphasized) at the Los Angeles Music and Arts School, in the heart of "East Los" as this community is affectionately called by some of its locals.

Ironically, my family had moved from its borders in 1965; I would return only to attend Catholic high school in the 1980's. Nevertheless, the umbilical cord was strong between those Chicanos who left its familiarity, bounded by its wide boulevards, ravines filled with cacti and chickens, intricate spiderweb of freeways, graffitied bridges along the LA River. I was "born in East LA" (as Cheech sang) to a proud Chicano family, who pulled up stakes from their home off Whittier Boulevard, by the time I walked. Following a caravan led by matriarch, Grandma Mary, my family moved to suburban San Gabriel Valley (still zoned for horses, with lower property taxes). My Grandma Mary later confided that their next-door neighbor on Clela Avenue would wander intoxicated, in the nude, on his side of the fence. Sunbathing, drunk or not, did not sit well with my devoutly Catholic abuela, whose earnest search for a new nest landed her in South San Gabriel.

In December of 1970, my mother drove us in our navy Plymouth Satellite from our tidy duplex on Elizabeth Avenue in Monterey Park, to East Los and its unlikely performing arts class. We cruised Garvey Avenue, took a left at Monterey Pass Road (where coyotes once roamed), past La Colonial Tortilleria (where we bought flour tortillas in bulk and my travieso little brother memorably pinched his finger on their assembly line machinery, then proceeded to howl like a coyote). Onward towards the Maravilla housing projects decorated with the brilliant hues of Our Lady of Guadalupe, the jai-alai courts and baseball field of Belvedere Park, finally we arrived at the Los Angeles School of Music and Art (LAMusArt) on Third Street.

This experimental class for "Eastside" preschoolers, was led by Pamela Collier, graduate of the Guildhall School of Music and Drama and Royal Academy of Music. The article described the curriculum as "…oriented toward achievement in dancing and acting, as well as good speech…" Later in life my curiosity got the best of me, discovering its alumni included: Sir James Galway, Daniel Craig, Ewan McGregor, and Michelle Dockery. As London's original municipal college, Guildhall School offers a fine arts higher education to the children of Britian's middle and working classes. Having learned Guildhall's history and mission, it made more sense to me why Ms. Collier volunteered her time and talents to children, at what was then considered an "inner city" performing arts school. She followed the footsteps of another artist, the actor Eartha Kitt, who founded a South-Central LA performing art academy, in the wake of the 1965 Watts riots. Perhaps Ms. Collier was the daughter of a grocer or lorry driver, and transcended her working-class origins by means of her higher education… and in an act of solidarity or plain generosity, she taught a cohort of diverse children in East LA, during the Christmas of 1970. A new decade ripe with expectations. With hope. It is interesting that the names and addresses of each student were printed in the article. Such a disclosure would be unheard of fifty years later. This was the era that began with front page headlines of the Manson trial. Neither the "Nightstalker," or "Hillside Strangler" were commonplace yet in the lexicon of Los Angeles press, nor were children's faces displayed on the sides of milk cartons.

I really do not have a clear recollection of Ms. Collier. I do remember the school, as though part of my early consciousness, and ballet classes, which did not last long. Something to do my inability to understand how to master "baby steps" and the unhappy realization that I would not begin lessons en pointe with satin slippers as I had seen in *The Red Shoes*. Nevertheless, my childhood was filled with sometimes challenging, always welcome diversion of dance: Ballet Folklorico with Anne Schwartz and her monotone New York accent; more Folklorico, Flamenco and Azteca dance with Sally Saavedra (who had studied under Rita Hayworth's instructor), culminating with instruction at UCLA's College of Fine Arts.

I honor my teachers such as Pamela Collier... as well as my Chicana mother for having infused my childhood with art's heady scent, which I adorned myself with for the rest of my life. Weekends at Huntington Gardens, sitting in silence with my mom, Gainsborough's *Blue Boy*, and Sir Thomas Lawrence's *Pinkie*, gave me a peaceful heart that I did not know I could possess, when my father's bipolar disorder was in full swing back home. Bored stiff on summer afternoons, I would secretly dance on my tiptoes until they burned against Grandma's green shag carpet, swaying to the *Blue Danube* on the Hi-Fi, transporting me to the Vienna woods.

In 1984, as a college Freshman, I participated in a fundraiser for the Los Angeles Music and Arts School. Somewhere in a shoebox within an East LA closet, there sits a photo of myself and another ELAC student: a statuesque engineering student, with a striking resemblance to Jessica Rabbit, sandwiched between the "Rhinestone Cowboy" Glen Campbell and Bob Hope in smart tuxedos. What I recall thinking when I met Mr. Campbell, was that he was blessed with talent, good looks, a quiet demeanor, and a generous heart for attending this event. I sighed, "The Adonis from Arkansas." What can I say, I was just nineteen with a penchant for handsome güeros. I suppose my peer group at the time may have assumed that this white, wealthy, extraordinarily successful performing artist, may not have given two cents about the artistic enrichment of minority children, yet he did. This sharecropper's son had quietly supported the Los Angeles Music and Arts School (LAMusArt), as did Bob and Dolores Hope, and Ms. Collier.

Since 1945, its mission has been to offer accessible, affordable arts education to children from all over Los Angeles County (Affordable Arts and Music Education | Los Angeles Music and Art School (lamusart.org). Benefactors such as these impacted the lives of generations of children who may not otherwise have been exposed to the performing arts, like me. We were taught to imagine, to create, to believe in possibilities, and attain dreams through the discipline inherent in the study of performing arts.

Memory and history both have utility in the healing journey. Whatever the connotations of a given history: honor it, learn the lesson, and move forward. In the process, we should not forget those who strived for positive change on behalf of the greater good, such as the artists…and the madres with dreams of a creative life for their children, which the East Los Angeles of 1970 could not contain. To do so would be a disservice.

In our recollections, my brothers and I did not remember feeling underprivileged or "poor" when we participated and found enjoyment in the arts during our childhoods; we felt welcomed into its experiential beauty and exhilarated at times by the organic process of creative expression. We felt fortunate, abundant in our inheritance, as in LAMusArt's goal to provide "creative paths and creative future," for imaginative little souls we were, and the human beings we were yet to become.

Mom's Surprise
BY S. J. PERRY

After ancient Greek pottery with gorgon

Skinny Jimmy was such a picky eater he was practically starving himself. Exasperated, desperate, his mom was open to any possible remedy.

One morning, the Today Show playing unheeded in the background, she scrolled the Etsy website, where she found a vintage bowl she thought might spark Jimmy's puny desire to eat. "Fun antique child's gorgon head bowl," the description read. "Your child will never fuss at mealtime again." She dug her credit card out of her purse and made the purchase.

A few days later, the box arrived on the porch, and Mom couldn't wait for Jimmy to open it. "Come here, Jimmy," she said, "I have a surprise for you that'll help you enjoy eating again."

"I doubt it, Mom," Jimmy whined, but he took the box and began ripping off the tape. He pulled out a wad of tissue and began to unfurl it. Suddenly he went quiet and still.

"What's wrong?" asked his mom. Jimmy didn't reply.

When Mom took a look at the gorgon glazed on the inside of the bowl, she too turned to stone.

Car Dancing

by Susan Posiviata

on the freeway
random radio streaming
turn it up loud   blasting
blue sky wind whipped
valley on a winter's day
mountains snow capped
crisped and chiseled
flexing their glory resounding
the joy of the perfect song
vibrating in my own personal
decompression chamber
toasty warm while the wind wails
my hands wave lips belting
merging with the flow of traffic
merging with my fellow travelers
in rhythm and space flowing
with the speed of our Earth
whose time is tick tick tick ticking
we have just 89 seconds
until the Doomsday Clock hits midnight
so I will accept this
4 minute gift of happiness
breathless and in awe

First Kiss

by Susan Posiviata

On a cool day in the middle of hot summer,
my best friend and I strolled down the street.
I was twelve, awkward and gangly, with wild frizzy hair
that did what it wanted and pubescent skin that erupted
in pimples whenever it wanted and I was yearning for adventure,
yearning to grow up, yearning for something I couldn't name.
We stopped to talk to a boy we knew
with dark hair and big brown eyes.
He wore a flannel shirt and his yard was strewn with car parts,
an old refrigerator, a trailer where his alcoholic uncle lived.
We talked and smoked and drank a little
as fat drops fell intermittently and low rumbles of thunder echoed.
When it was time to go my friend delicately faded away
as I stood there without the faintest idea of who I was
or what I wanted. I can't remember his name only
that he was lean and strong and had lips like flint
that sparked a warm feeling, an electric feeling, an inexplicable
    feeling,
that even the summer rain falling in big wet splashes could not
    extinguish.
Later when my mother asked where I had been
and why was I wet, I told her I got caught in the rain
on the way home from my friend's house.
Then I sat down and I ate my dinner,
my secret source of happiness burning like a fire
inside me while I smiled and nodded and talked about the weather.

Little White Lies with a Purpose

BY LESLIE ROUNDY

She was scared. The room where she now hung her clothes and slept at night wasn't familiar to her at all. Who *were* these people who cheerfully greeted her every morning as she got dressed, and then returned at day's end to help her change into her nightgown and tuck her into a bed she didn't recognize? She didn't understand why she was eating with strangers in a room that seemed more like a family-run restaurant than a dining room in a home— people dressed alike serving meals to those at each table, a room decorated with fake plants and random pictures hanging on drab white walls.

I was scared. Have we made the right decision? She said numerous times that she never wanted to live in a place like this. Does she really need this level of care? She can still do some things on her own and she has me to help her. Will she be safe? Stories of elder abuse consumed my thoughts. How is she going to get along without me? She'll be so confused.

My siblings and I knew that the time had come to move Mom into a memory care facility. I wasn't ready emotionally, yet deep down I knew it was best for her well-being. It was time to pull the Band-Aid off.

Mom had come to live with me a few years earlier, uprooting a life she loved in the serene mountains of Arizona. In her mind, the move was necessary because I was living alone and working full time, and she would be able to help me out. Our family's concerns about her living alone hadn't been discussed with her. Nothing wrong with skewing the story a tad, right? Little did I know then that that would be the beginning of telling a fib now and then to protect her from the reality of growing older and living with a declining memory.

This move led to role reversal at its finest. I, the daughter, was now taking care of the mother. *My* mother. A sweet, funny, petite woman in her mid-80s whom I loved with all my heart, as I knew she loved me. I was the one in charge and making the decisions. It was time for *me* to protect *her*.

In those early weeks after moving into the facility, Mom would call me at night. With each question, I could hear the tremendous anxiety in her shaky, teary voice. "Where are you?" "Where am I?" "When can I go home?" "Can you come get me?" The word heartbreaking doesn't begin to describe how those calls made me feel. Sad. Guilty. Emotionally drained. Protecting her this time—from the fear—seemed unsurmountable.

I would visit often, taking my lunch break to see her or spending time with her on weekends where I'd encourage her to participate in activities, followed by lunch together in that drab dining room. When it came time for me to leave after each visit, she couldn't understand why I wasn't taking her home with me. She was filled with confusion; I could see it on her face and hear it in her voice. "When are you coming back?" I would quickly get up, give her a kiss on the cheek, tell her I love her, and leave. Rip the Band-Aid off. I took comfort in knowing that she would soon forget that I had been there and wouldn't remember the unsettling goodbye. This became our routine, and thankfully it eventually got easier for both of us.

I'd often hear the little white lies that other family members would tell their loved ones. "I'm just going to the bathroom. I'll be right back." "I have to go talk to someone in the office. I'll be right back." "I'm going to go get xyz out of your room. I'll be right back." This was their way of escaping a difficult goodbye.

I could never do that.

Or so I thought.

The day eventually came. I did it. I lied to my mother. "I'll be right back," I told her, knowing full well that our visit had come to an end. The instantaneous guilt. The sadness that washed through me as I walked to my car. The tears rolling down my cheeks. The comfort of a hug from Kim, a caring staff member I encountered in the parking lot. The anger at this disease called Alzheimer's.

Then I did it again. And again. Practice makes perfect, after all. "I'm going to go get your prescriptions filled. I'll be right back." "I'll come back later this afternoon, Mom." "We'll have to wait and see what Dr. Kang says about you going home." A healthy dose of Hope each time, served on a shiny silver platter. Hope that the life she once knew would become familiar to her again.

Truth: I would never be bringing her home. I knew that from the day I moved her into the facility. And as hard as it was, telling those fibs was for the best. I probably lied to Mom as a child, but this was different. I was doing it *for her*—to ease her mind and her anxiety. To reassure her that we'd spend time together again soon. That she would once again feel safe and at peace, fear no longer ruling her.

Faith

BY KRISTINE SHELL

I thought I knew some things back then –
some whats, some wheres, some whys, some whens,
some things to trust beyond my doubts.
But then, it seems, my doubts won out.
So now, I'm left to seek new truths,
to trust in things I cannot prove,
convinced there's light where darkness falls
a vantage point beyond these walls.

The Moment
BY MELISSA STARK

Lasting memory of that night
obscured silence broken by the rush of
gravity pulling tears down, crashing on my
affluent hands. These instruments play in five-thirty time
now take a breath…..again 2,3,4,5
Start compressions, all the way to thirty
this melody stuck on repeat, forcing
air to escape my lips
rushing, searching for a way to give you life, the
kinetic whisper of hope left cold
Deafening screams
I can never forget
Exactly when my broken heart continued to
Drum on and yours stopped

tinyurl.com/TheMomentASL

Violet the Artist

by Gudelia Vaden

Violet, or Didi, as she is usually called is my bonus grandchild along with her sibling, Kara. Her parents are my son, Patrick and his fiancée, Amanda. Violet, at three and Kara at seven years old live in Orangecrest which is five minutes from my home. I would on occasion be asked to babysit and was more than happy to. But would I, at 72 years of age be up for the task? I will admit it is challenging, as Violet is language delayed and cannot talk. The only word she can say is Didi and that is how she got her nickname. I am curious if she can express herself through art. She also has a short attention span, but could understand simple words such as, sit, eat and play.

Violet could sing in the most angelical voice you ever heard. She knew every word in the song, "Let it Go" and sang it flawlessly.

She enjoys coming over to my spacious home in Hillcrest. When I am not babysitting, I express my creativity by painting flowers, hummingbirds and sparrows that come to my backyard. I realize it is never too early to introduce Violet to the world of art. I begin by introducing her to finger painting with shaving cream and letting her feel the texture and smell the berry scented cream. Violet could not stop smiling from ear to ear, as she moves the shaving cream with her little hands, thus creating her first art. When Mom picks her up, she points to the table feeling proud of herself and gets a big hug from me and a bigger hug from Mom. Her bright smile tells me my first lesson is a success.

A week later, Kara mentions that she loves coming over with Violet and appreciates that I have included various art and craft supplies for them. It is almost Halloween, their favorite holiday. I place white paper, markers, child scissors and paper sacks for puppet making. Kara can cut with scissors, but Violet needs help.

I put a cotton ball in a Kleenex tissue and tie it with a small piece of yarn to make a ghost. Kara and Violet make several and take them home to hang on their patio. When the wind blows the ghosts come alive, as they flutter in the wind.

Time passes quickly. Violet is now four years old and her parents enroll her in a specialized preschool that focuses on language development. She will see a Speech therapist for a few hours each day. She takes the classes for a few months and her teacher believes she now uses words and makes sentences appropriate for her age. She graduates early. Her teachers notice that she is the first one to the art table, is very creative and ready for kindergarten.

We are so happy with the good news, especially that Violet cannot only express herself, but simply cannot stop talking. My husband and I decide to take her to her favorite place, McDonald's to celebrate. While there I forgot to bring paper to draw and hand Violet a napkin and lend her my pen. She decides to draw her family. She makes circles for the heads and rectangle shapes for the bodies. She puts a dress on herself, her mom and Kara and pants for her dad. I praise her for a job well done. She reminds me so much of a story about Einstein where he scribbled his math problems on a napkin.

Violet continues to sketch and draw and creates a self-portrait using bright colored markers and white paper. I show it to my daughter Natalie and her husband Rick and they decide to publish her art in Natalie's Zine, an online magazine for artists, poets and writers. Violet is becoming more confident about sharing her artwork. At seven and eight years old she watches Disney movies and draws the characters, such as Cinderella. and even makes her own story books and staples the pages, so they turn like a book.

When she is nine, she makes the cover of Natalie's Zine by drawing a king and queen using water colors and markers. This made me so proud; the tears of joy keep cascading down my face.

I do not know if she realizes that this is a high honor that her drawing was selected. All she knows is that she loves to draw and paint just like her grandma Delia.

Love Letter to Riverside: Historical Spanish and Mexican Influences

BY FRANCES J. VÁSQUEZ

A public museum in Riverside began with a bountiful gift. Mary Elizabeth Rumsey donated a collection of 600 Native artifacts to the City of Riverside that she and her late husband Cornelius Earle Rumsey collected during their travels. Thanks to the foundational Rumsey gift in 1924, the Riverside City Council established the Cornelious Earle Rumsey Indian Museum. It was housed at City Hall for public display. A century later and throughout 2024, the Museum of Riverside celebrated its 100th year anniversary with various public activities and events, including an amazing exhibition, "Dear Riverside, a letter to our first love." The exhibition opened on July 25, 2024 to express how the museum shows its love for the community through stewardship, exhibitions, and community programming*. Because the museum's main facility was closed for renovations, the exhibition was held at Riverside City College's Center for Social Justice and Civil Liberties. The Museum of Riverside exhibited my love letter at the centennial exhibition:

Querido Riverside:

Local history was enriched by Spanish and Mexican influences. In 1774 - 76, los Españoles led by Capitan Juan Bautista de Anza from Sonora, México encountered friendly indigenous peoples called Tongva, Cahuilla, Wa'achen, Serrano, and Luiseño. During these explorations, they designated Spanish names for the rivers, mountains, deserts, and landmarks they encountered. In 1838 Juan Bandini was granted Rancho Jurupa which lay on both sides of the Santa Ana River. In 1842, Lorenzo Trujillo began to bring families from New Mexico via the Old Spanish Trail. The early settlers appreciated the gentle river and fertile sandy loam that produced abundant fruits, vegetables, and prize-winning citrus trees.

My father, Leonard Vasquez, worked as mayordomo (manager) for LVW Brown Estate in Highgrove, where Mexicanos lived and worked hard in harmony with verdant orange groves. In the summer, kids cooled off in the Gage canals that irrigated local citrus. During freezing temperatures, my dad and workers toiled to ignite the smudge pots installed among the citrus groves to keep the fruit from freezing. The heavy smoke emissions blackened our nostrils and stained the yellow walls of our kitchen with an oily black veil. On workdays (Monday-Saturday) my dad drove a company truck to pick up laborers to harvest citrus fruit. After arduous work, he returned them to their destinations. He began in Highgrove followed by stops in South Colton and the Fairmount Park labor camp to pick up los Braceros.

Braceros were initially recruited from México as guest workers to provide agricultural work during WWII to address the labor shortage created by the war overseas. Braceros lived in labor camps and were often lonely. On occasional Sundays, my dad invited Braceros to our home in Highgrove to help with projects and offered them friendly hospitality and home-cooked meals prepared by my mother. We all spoke Spanish so los Braceros had a good time.

My Tía Margarita and Uncle Peter owned numerous acres of citrus groves in Riverside. She served hand-squeezed orange juice at her stand on Iowa and 8th Street in Riverside. She sold a portion of her property to the Regents of the University of California to build a new campus.

Viva UCR!

My love for the Museum began during a school field trip in the 1950s where I admired the amazing Butterfly collection and native artifacts, particularly the spectacular baskets. My love is nurtured by informative present-day lectures, programs and exhibitions like the mini-museum in Casa Blanca. I love how the museum has maintained the beautiful Heritage House on Magnolia Avenue and the iconic Harada House on Lemon Street. It would be lovely to acquire a typical warehouse to depict how the citrus fruit was packed for commerce.

Like the Monarch Butterflies from Michoacán, Mexicanos migrated from Revolutionary War-torn México, including my paternal grandparents, among others. Ysabel Solorio Olvera joined her husband to raise a family in Casa Blanca and led a valiant petition in 1911 for the school board to build a neighborhood school. The struggle for education equity resulted in a new school and a civically engaged community.

Te Amo Riverside,

Frances J. Vasquez

*The Centennial exhibition opened with a reception on July 25, 2024 and was on display until January 5, 2025. Museum staff did a superb job of interpreting the breadth and depth of the collection and highlighted its close relationship with the community.

NOTE: Two intrepid Mexican women from Casa Blanca presented a petition at a Riverside City Board of Education meeting to request a neighborhood school for their children. Accompanied by their husbands and neighbors, they walked over four miles in the summer heat. The group led by Ysabel Solorio Olvera and her "comadre" served as Casa Blanca's culture bearers in pursuit of educational equity. Sadly, the women's names were not recorded in the minutes, nor in the newspaper report the next day. Diligent research has not yet revealed the comadre's name.

The minutes of the July 11, 1911, Board meeting state, "A petition was presented signed by eighty residents of Casa Blanca, asking for the erection of a public school in that locality. It appears that more than seventy children of school age reside in Casa Blanca: that forty children in primary grades now go to Victoria School." The District established makeshift classrooms in 1913 for kindergarten and first grade in an abandoned warehouse. They moved the old wooden structure in 1918 to Madison Street, where it later burned. A new Casa Blanca School was finally erected in 1923. But, against the wishes of the Casa Blanca community, the District closed it in 1967 to implement a desegregation school busing program that exists to date. After decades-long advocacy by community leaders, a new state-of-the-art Casa Blanca School is under construction with plans to open in school year 2025.

ADDENDUM: With the signing of the Treaty of Cordova in 1821, México gained its independence from Spain and California became Mexican territory. The Mexican Republic established the Secularization Act of 1833 and began a series of privately owned rancho land grants which were made throughout the state. In 1838, California governor José Figueroa, granted Juan Bandini a seven-square-league Rancho Jurupa encompassing both sides of the Santa Ana River. In 1842, Juan Bandini and Benjamin D. Wilson invited New Mexico colonists led by Lorenzo Trujillo from Abiquiu to protect the ranchos from horse raiders with the promise of giving them 2200 acres — the Bandini Donation. Traveling on the Old Spanish Trail on foot, they initially settled in Politana [near present-day San Bernardino Valley Community College] at the behest of the owners of Rancho San Bernardino, particularly Vicente Lugo.

About 1843-45, the Trujillo settlers established the community of Agua Mansa further down along the Santa Ana River. Don Benito Wilson apportioned each man an individual farm lot as part of the Bandini Donation. Louis Rubidoux purchased the 6700-acre Rubidoux Rancho. The early settlers appreciated the area's gentle flowing river and fertile sandy loam and built homes with the adobe bricks they made from the earth. They excavated zanjas (ditches) to irrigate their crops, which in combination with the sunny climate, produced abundant fruits, vegetables, and fruit/nut trees. It was said that the maíz grew as tall as any man!

In 1848, the Treaty of Guadalupe was signed after the United States war with México and California became U.S. territory. In 1862, Agua Mansa was flooded by the rain-swollen Santa Ana River. People sought refuge at San Salvador, referred to as Spanish Town by local Anglos. The New Mexico settlers established La Placita de los Trujillos near Highgrove where they cultivated farmlands with the irrigation ditches they excavated. Years later, the entire region was abundant with citrus groves that would produce prize-winning oranges. In 1870, the city of Riverside was founded and was so named because of its location near the Santa Ana River. Later in 1893, the city was selected as the County Seat of Riverside.

In 1875 at La Placita, the Trujillos established an adobe one-room school. They hired Alice Rowan in 1888 to teach at the school. She was an African American daughter of free slaves who migrated to San Bernardino on a Mormon wagon train. Miss Rowan graduated from the State Normal School for teachers in Los Angeles [now UCLA]. She was the first Black certificated teacher in California.

The University of California at Riverside main campus is located near Box Springs Mountain, east of downtown Riverside and south of neighboring Highgrove (originally called East Riverside by the colonists). The original buildings included the UC Citrus Experiment Station, residential buildings, and a barn. Groundbreaking was held in April 1951 for the College of Humanities, Arts and Social Sciences (CHASS). Five buildings were completed by 1954 and UCR was declared a "general campus" of the UC system in 1958.

Te amo, UCR — my Alma Mater!

Trapped

BY GABRIEL VASQUEZ

I followed a spider
Under my bed
I asked Mrs. Spider
Where is your web?
I've ran out of silk
There's nothing to eat
I need something sweet
To continue my feat
I flew outside and
Asked Mr. Fly
I have a good friend
I'd like you to meet.

13

BY GABRIEL VASQUEZ

I stepped on a crack
And never looked back
I crossed under a ladder
And said what's the matter?
I spilled all the salt
And swept it away
I cracked all the mirrors
And started to say
Bad Luck isn't real
It's something they say
Don't cross your fingers
And hope it's okay

Contributor Bios

Susan M. Rump Abir is a Creative Writer of Distinction from Riverside Community College and a first generation college graduate of CSUSB. Susan's poetry has won several awards including being published in *Muse*. Her short fiction was included in an *Annenberg Anthology*. In 2023-24 she traveled across Europe while freelancing. She recently received publication for the poem "Spooning" at the WILDsound writing festival. (Essay Writing Boot Camp with J.D. Mathes)

Janet Lako Alexander is a poet, writer, and bilingual educator. A UC Riverside graduate, she was born in Blythe and raised in Rubidoux, California. Her works have appeared in *Writing from Inlandia* and other publications. She teaches poetry writing/performance for the Ontario-Montclair School District. (Writing for Children with Jose Chavez, All Genres Workshop/Honoring our Ancestors with James Coats, Micro Memoir with David Puma, Art and Craft of Poetry with Romaine Washington, Ekphrastic Bootcamp with John Brantingham, Poet-TRY Bootcamp with Stephanie Barbé Hammer)

Margit Andersson was born in Sweden and has lived in Hemet for the last 20 years. She has always been interested in literature and in writing. (Mae Wagner's Joslyn Joy Writers)

Eric Barr taught acting and directing and was the Chairman of the UCR Theatre Department. He created UCR's MFA in Creative Writing and Writing for the Performing Arts. He was the Artistic Director of the Porthouse Theatre and taught at the Stella Adler Conservatory, and worked as an acting coach with the National Theatre of the Deaf. Since surviving a series of strokes Barr has written a one-man show about his surgeries, hospitalizations, and rehab. Check out his podcasts on stroke recovery can be found at http/www.apieceofmymind.net (John Brantingham's flash fiction & manuscript prep workshops)

Karen Bradford, M.A., is an award-winning writer and photographer and presently a three-term elected board of education trustee. She also is a director on the board of the community cultural and historical treasure, The Jurupa Mountains Discovery Center. She was the public relations manager for *The Press-Enterprise* and a campus communications officer at the University of California, Riverside. She is an ace editor and has written two books of local nonfiction history and is previously published in Inlandia anthologies. (Wil Clarke's Celena's Scribes)

Mary Briggs is a first-generation Mexican American. She was born in 1939 to a family of migrant workers and raised in East Los Angeles. Mary has resided in Riverside since 1991. (Rose Monge's Writing Warriors at the Janet Goeske Center)

Patty Brown started attending the Redlands Joslyn Joy Writers with Mae Marinello when she retired. At first she only intended to sit, watch, and listen. Mae said, "No way", tossed her a notebook, and said, "Write!" The workshop has become like family and is a regular part of the week. (Mae Wagner's Joslyn Joy Writers)

Stephanie Bruce has written songs and poems all her life. Eight years ago, she expanded her writing into short stories, fiction and non-fiction. She says whether it's writing fiction, non-fiction, poetry or song...putting heart to pen and pen to paper is a magical process. One that she enjoys daily. (Mae Wagner's Joslyn Joy Writers)

Georgette Geppert Buckley In the year 2024, Georgette had the privilege to continue with Wil's Celena Scribes as well as the endeavor to write Byzantine style Iconography. She dedicates her writings to her mother's memory who has been her cheerleader, art patron and role model. (Wil Clarke's Celena's Scribes)

Bridgette Callahan raised her family in the Inland Empire, where she earned various degrees at Riverside CC and CSU-San Bernardino. She has taught writing at the University of Redlands for twelve years, and her writing has appeared in *Pacific REVIEW, The Beacon, Writing from Inlandia,* and *Inlandia: A Literary Journey.* (Honoring Our Ancestors Poetry Workshop with James Coats and All Genres Workshop with James Coats)

Darcel Cannady is a retired School Counselor. From the written word, to sign language, to musical scores, to chirping birds, to shadows dancing in the leaf-light, to sun rises and moon sets, she listens as the world speaks softly, communicating God's love. (Mae Wagner Marinello's Joslyn Joy Writers)

Ellen Cantor uses poetry to interpret her feelings and to examine how events impact her life. Ellen received a BS from The University of Illinois at Champaign-Urbana and continued her education in Interior and Architectural Design at UCLA. She has studied poetry through Inlandia and with Nancy Woo. (Victoria Waddle's All-Genres Workshop)

Alben Chamberlain is a retired middle and high school teacher. He has lived in the Inland Empire for most of his life. He is a former Navy Reserve Officer and Retirement Counselor. He is married and has three children and four grandchildren. (Wil Clarke's Celena's Scribes and Romaine Washington's the Art and Craft of Writing Poetry)

Natalie Michele Champion participated in the Chronologyland workshops. She is a poet and teacher. She is from Riverside, but lives in San Francisco with her husband Rick and cat Milo Morris. (Carlos Cortés' Chronologyland)

Rick Champion is a mathematician in exile-turned-writer. He publishes *Natalie's Zine* together with companions as guided by the Muse. The Zine appears occasionally, which is to say every now and then. (Carlos Cortés' Chronologyland)

As an avid reader, **Sylvia Clarke** has enjoyed writing since early in her life. Now that she is retired, she finds short memoir pieces her favorite stories to write. She also loves singing and started voice lessons in her 80th year. (Rose Monge's Writing Warriors and Wil Clarke's Celena's Scribes)

Wil Clarke is looking forward to publishing his memoir on five years spent in Tanzania, East Africa. He enjoys participating in Rose Monge's Memoir writing workshop, and Carlos Cortés's

Chronologyland, and facilitating Celena's Scribes Workshop. He grew up in Africa and has lived in Riverside since 1986. (Carlos Cortés' Chronologyland, Rose Monge's Writing Warriors, and Wil Clarke's Celena's Scribes)

James Coats is an award winning author, poet and educator from Southern California. You can take a poetry workshop with him through his organization Lift Our Voices Education which hosts an award winning workshop monthly called Be The Change: Social Justice Writing Workshop. He's a 2023 Poetry Pushcart Prize nominee. (All Genres Workshop with James Coats)

Elinor Cohen wanted to be an astronomer but couldn't commit to all the math. So instead she got a degree in Pre-Modern Literature that she never uses. Elinor resides with family in the desolate desert after decades as an Angeleno, and is fully obsessed with her rescue dog Floof. (Breathing Life Into Characters with Renee Gurley, ASL Poetry with Ryan Fingerle, All Genres Workshop with Victoria Waddle)

Hilda Cruz is a transformational Latina leader, an immigrant justice advocate, and a spiritual coach dedicated to nurturing the hearts of social justice leaders. Formerly the Regional Program Director at the Interfaith Movement for Human Integrity, she grounds her work in her lived experience as a first-generation Mexican immigrant. A mother, wife, grandmother, friend, and mentor, she embodies the resilience, stories, and spiritual beauty of her culture every day. (Honoring Our Ancestors Poetry Workshop with James Coats)

Chuck Doolittle has enjoyed attending the Joslyn Joy Writer's workshop for about three years now. He specifically has appreciated the great writers in the group, as they have encouraged and inspired him to greater heights. (Mae Wagner Marinello's Joslyn Joy Writers)

Reiss DuPlessis is a native of New Orleans but lives happily in Southern California. (Wil Clarke's Celena's Scribes)

Jerry Ellingson lives in Redlands, California. She is a retired teacher with a bachelor's degree in dance and English. Her master's degree is in Education. The greatest joys in her life have been teaching Graphic Design and Computer to adults and her role as a mother and grandmother. (Mae Wagner Marinello's Joslyn Joy Writers)

Bryan Franco is a neurodivergent, gay, Jewish poet from Brunswick, Maine. He is published in Australia, Canada, Chile, England, Germany, Holland, India, Ireland, Scotland, and the US. Bryan hosts Café Generalissimo open mic. He is an artist and culinary genius. His book, *Everything I Think Is All in My Mind*, was published in 2021. (Wil Clarke's Celena's Scribes)

Nan Friedley is a retired special education teacher. Her poetry has been published in a chapbook, *Short Bus Ride* by Bad Knee Press, *Indiana Voice Journal,* and *Writing from Inlandia* anthologies. (Romaine Washington's the Art and Craft of Writing Poetry and Writing for Children with José Chavez)

Ginger M. Galloway earned her BA from Azusa Pacific University and teaches elementary school part-time. In her free time she enjoys crocheting, knitting, doll-making, and reading. She is co-founder of Wild Seed Poetry and Arts Collective providing creative spaces and opportunities for poets, writers, and artists of color. (James Coats Persona Poem/Selfie Poetry at RAM)

Camille Gaon is a lover of anything literary and unleashes her imagination daily to indulge in unsubdued storytelling. She has written and performed pieces at The Wallis Annenberg Center for Performing Arts in Beverly Hills and at The Broad Stage in Santa Monica even though she can't act. (Wil Clarke's Celena's Scribes)

Chris "The Poetic Genius" Green is a thirty-eight-year-old poet from Gloucester, Virginia. For twenty-four years, The Poetic Genius has been working to perfect his craft, using it to empower himself and his community through poems exploring his African American heritage, his family history, and his own life experiences. (Romaine Washington's the Art and Craft of Writing Poetry)

Mark Grinyer published poems in *Rattle, The Main Street Rag, The Literary Review, The Pacific Review, Perigee*, etc. A chapbook, *Approaching Poetry*, is available from Finishing Line Press and Amazon. He received a PhD in English from U.C.R. Now retired, he lives on the edge of the Cleveland National Forest. (Romaine Washington's the Art and Craft of Writing Poetry)

Milan Hamilton has been a participant in a weekly writing group for more than fifteen years, half of those in the Inlandia Joslyn Joy Writers ongoing creative writing workshop led by Mae Marinello. He has lived in Redlands since 1979 and studies and writes poetry and short stories. (Mae Wagner Marinello's Joslyn Joy Writers)

Beverly Head is a retired professor and poet, and author of *Walking North*, winner of the Naomi Long Madgett Poetry Award. (Romaine Washington's the Art and Craft of Writing Poetry)

Richard "Rich" Hess is a retired physician. He practiced Obstetrics/Gynecology in Fairbanks, Alaska for 41 years. He is now living in Springdale, Arkansas with his wife, Marie. He enjoys writing about his medical and other life experiences. (Mae Wagner Marinello's Joslyn Joy Writers)

Connie Jameson, a retired elementary and special education teacher, enjoys reading, writing, travel, nature, antiques, theater and Toastmasters. Her first published book was *Dating 'n' Mating: Wit and Wisdom on Love and Marriage*. Connie has three published children's picture books, *Twinkle Toes, Slow Down, Tommy Turtle* and *MaryBelle's Special Spot*. (Wil Clarke's Celena's Scribes)

Caecilia (CeCe) Johns was born near Munich, Germany in 1934. CeCe was a witness to many of the heartbreaking happenings of World War II. She moved to the United States and became a citizen in 1968. She lives in Yucaipa, California. (Mae Wagner Marinello's Joslyn Joy Writers)

Margo Klein is a retired CPA. She joined Joslyn Joy Writers at the urging of a friend and found the joy of writing. (Mae Wagner Marinello's Joslyn Joy Writers)

Robin Longfield was born in Atlanta, GA, but grew up in Northwestern Orange County, in pre "The O.C." days. She has lived in the Inland Empire longer than anywhere else. She believes in magic, possibilities, and adventures. She is forever grateful for her family, friends, teachers, and workshop leaders. (Honoring Our Ancestors with James Coats, All Genres with Victoria Waddle)

James Luna is the author of *The Runaway Piggy/El Cochinito Fugitivo*, *A Mummy in Her Backpack/Una momia en su mochila*, and *The Place Where You Live/El lugar donde vives*, and *Growing Up on the Playground/Nuestro patio de recreo* all published by Piñata Books, Arte Público Press. Piggy was awarded the 2012 Tejas Star Award as chosen by the students of the Rio Grande Valley of Texas. James has taken part in panels and readings at the Texas Book Festival, the Latino Book and Family Festival and the California Association for Bilingual Education conference. He has presented at schools in Southern California and Texas. He is a member of SCBWI. James participated and thoroughly enjoyed Inlandia's Micro Memoir class with David Puma. James lives in Riverside, California. (David Puma's Micro Memoir)

Merrill Lyew is retired; he practices a few hobbies like solving chess problems, drafting short-short stories, taking snapshots, walking, etc. (Mae Wagner Marinello's Joslyn Joy Writers)

Anne Malcolm is an immigrant of English descent. She spent her childhood in Kenya. Anne holds a BSc in Plant Science from UC Riverside, she is a Phi Beta Kappa scholar and worked in Landscape Design and Plant Breeding. She is grateful to live with her children in Redlands California. (Mae Wagner Marinello's Joslyn Joy Writers and James Coats' Honoring Our Ancestors)

Mae Wagner Marinello has been a part of Inlandia since 2008. She began facilitating a weekly workshop at the Joslyn Senior Center in Redlands in 2014. When the pandemic hit, the Joslyn Joy Writers began meeting via Zoom. Mae lives in Redlands with her joyful little dog named Cricket. (Mae Wagner Marinello's Joslyn Joy Writers)

Elisse Martinez was born in Buffalo, NY, and moved to Riverside in 1970 with her family. She received her Master of Education at Hunter College, and Special Ed Credential from UCR. Elisse came to writing at the age of 80, inspired by Renée Gurley's "Show, Don't Tell" writing classes. (Show, Don't Tell with Renee Gurley)

Terry Lee Marzell lives in Chino Hills, California. Now retired, she taught school for 36 years. She earned her BA in English from CSUF, her MA in Interdisciplinary Studies from CSUSB, and a Library Science credential from CSULB. Terry has published two books about remarkable teachers and one YA novel. (Mae Wagner Marinello's Joslyn Joy Writers)

Rose Y. Monge has facilitated the memoir class at the Goeske Center since 2009. She encourages others to write their life story as it can be therapeutic and healing. It also may be inspirational and educational for the reader. She advocates for social justice, diversity and inclusion in the community. (Rose Y. Monge's Writing Warriors at the Janet Goeske Senior Center)

Barbara Mortensen is a retired former executive who likes to write mainly memoir and essays and loves the Inlandia Institute Writing Workshops. (Wil Clarke's Celena's Scribes, Personal Essay Boot Camp with Jerry Mathes, and Victoria Waddle's All-Genres Writing Workshop)

Savannah Muñoz is a Southern California writer with work published in *OC Weekly* and *Claremont Courier*. She recently graduated from UC San Diego with a degree in Literature/Writing and specializes in content writing and copy editing. (Victoria Waddle's All-Genres Writing Workshop)

Gary Neuharth lives in Redlands, California. He is a member of the Joslyn Joy Writers Group. He has formally studied art, sculpture and writing and been inspired by Venice Beach, California, the Bohemian life, and the Beat Generation. Gary has published more than a hundred poems. (Mae Wagner Marinello's Joslyn Joy Writers)

Deborah Nevárez is a Chicana who was born and raised in East Los Angeles, a UCLA graduate, mother of three adult sons, a Second-Degree black belt in Taekwondo, and breast cancer survivor. She serves the community as a psychotherapist and is currently writing a family memoir. (Personal Essay Boot Camp with Jerry Mathes)

S. J. Perry is the author of *Soul*, a poetry chapbook (Arroyo Seco). His work has appeared in *Cholla Needles, Last Leaves*, and elsewhere. He studied at Emporia State University and the University of Kansas. A retired high school English teacher, he lives in Southern California's San Gorgonio Pass. (Ekphrastic Bootcamp with John Brantingham and Jane Edberg)

Susan Posiviata recently retired after 37 years of teaching. She is now free to devote herself to her other lifelong passion of writing poetry. Susan writes about growing up in San Bernardino, anxiety, and the chaotic but beautiful world in which we live. (David Puma's Spoken Word Poetry and Micro Memoir, James Coats' All Genres Workshop, and Romaine Washington's The Art and Craft of Writing Poetry)

Leslie Roundy is a long-time resident of Redlands. She used her writing skills throughout her career in marketing and human resources. Now that she is retired, Leslie is pursuing her passion for writing by participating in Inlandia workshops and writing for nonprofits. She also volunteers with the Joslyn Senior Center. (All Genres Workshops with James Coats)

Kristine Shell lives in Redlands, California, where she participates in the Joslyn Writers Group and the Inlandia Institute. Kristine is a retired school administrator and teacher. She holds Bachelor of Arts degrees in English and Secondary Education. She also holds Master of Education degrees in Elementary Reading and School Administration. (Mae Wagner Marinello's Joslyn Joy Writers)

Melissa Stark is a proud mom of two beautiful children. She is an advocate for epilepsy awareness and seizure first aid. She is currently enrolled in an ASL interpreter program with a passion for communication. Melissa had the pleasure of attending the ASL poetry workshop in the Fall of 2024. (ASL Poetry with Ryan Fingerle)

Gudelia "Delia" Vaden, is a teacher, poet, writer and artist. Her writings reflect her love of nature and writing. She illustrates and contributes to *Natalie's Zine*, an on-line magazine. While teaching, she earned a BA Degree from California State University, San Bernardino. (Rose Y. Monge's Writing Warriors at Janet Goeske Senior Center and Carlos Cortés' Chronologyland)

Frances J. Vásquez is native to the Inland region and attended local schools: Highgrove Elementary, University Heights JH, Poly HS, RCC and UCR. She serves as Director Emerita of Inlandia Institute and various committees. An aficionada of arts and letters, she is passionate about Celebrating Cultura and local history. (Show, Don't Tell with Renee Gurley)

Gabriel Vasquez is a student at RCC and full time mechanic. He writes poetry in his free time and is working towards a degree in English. (Bonnie Hearn Hill Character driven suspense fiction)

About Inlandia Institute

Inlandia Institute is a regional literary non-profit and publishing house. We seek to bring focus to the richness of the literary enterprise that has existed in this region for ages. The mission of the Inlandia Institute is to recognize, support, and expand literary activity in all of its forms in Inland Southern California by publishing books and sponsoring programs that deepen people's awareness, understanding, and appreciation of this unique, complex and creatively vibrant region.

The Institute publishes books, presents free public literary and cultural programming, provides in-school and after school enrichment programs for children and youth, holds free creative writing workshops for teens and adults, and boot camp intensives. In addition, every two years, the Inlandia Institute appoints a distinguished jury panel from outside of the region to name an Inlandia Literary Laureate who serves as an ambassador for the Inlandia Institute, promoting literature, creative literacy, and community. Laureates to date include Susan Straight (2010-2012), Gayle Brandeis (2012-2014), Juan Delgado (2014-2016), Nikia Chaney (2016-2018), and Rachelle Cruz (2018-2020).

To learn more about the Inlandia Institute, please visit our website at www.InlandiaInstitute.org.

Inlandia Books